FLIGHT FROM
A LADY

The following titles are all in the *Fonthill Complete A. G. Macdonell* Series.
The year indicates when the first edition was published.
See **www.fonthillmedia.com** for details.

Fiction

England, their England	(1933)
How Like an Angel	(1934)
Lords and Masters	(1936)
The Autobiography of a Cad	(1939)
Flight From a Lady	(1939)
Crew of the Anaconda	(1940)

Short Stories

The Spanish Pistol	(1939)

Non-Fiction

Napoleon and his Marshals	(1934)
A Visit to America	(1935)
My Scotland	(1937)

Crime and Thrillers written under the pseudonym of John Cameron

The Seven Stabs	(1929)
Body Found Stabbed	(1932)

Crime and Thrillers written under the pseudonym of Neil Gordon

The New Gun Runners	(1928)
The Factory on the Cliff	(1928)
The Professor's Poison	(1928)
The Silent Murders	(1929)
The Big Ben Alibi	(1930)
Murder in Earl's Court	(1931)
The Shakespeare Murders	(1933)

FLIGHT FROM
A LADY

A. G. MACDONELL

FONTHILL

To
The Lady
of course

Fonthill Media Limited
Fonthill Media LLC
www.fonthillmedia.com
office@fonthillmedia.com

First published 1939
This edition published in the United Kingdom 2012

British Library Cataloguing in Publication Data:
A catalogue record for this book is available from the British Library

ISBN 978-1-78155-020-5 (print)
ISBN 978-1-78155-159-2 (e-book)

Typeset in 11pt on 14pt Sabon.
Printed and bound in England

Contents

Introduction
To The 2012 Edition

As a writer, A. G. Macdonell was fortunate to reach his prime at such a pivotal moment in the history of the human race. In 1939, when Macdonell wrote *Flight from a Lady*, a fictional travelogue charting the adventures of a fleeing inamorato across Europe, the Middle East, and India, the world was on the brink of upheaval; few contemporary novelists saw more clearly what was to come.

Archibald Gordon Macdonell — Archie — was born on 3 November 1895 in Poona, India, the younger son of William Robert Macdonell of Mortlach, a prominent merchant in Bombay, and Alice Elizabeth, daughter of John Forbes White, classical scholar and patron of the arts. It seems likely that Archie was named after Brevet-Colonel A. G. Macdonell, CB, presumably an uncle, who commanded a force that defeated Sultan Muhammed Khan at the fort of Shabkader in the Afghan campaign of 1897.

The family left India in 1896 and Archie was brought up at 'Colcot' in Enfield, Middlesex, and the Macdonell family home of 'Bridgefield', Bridge of Don, Aberdeen. He was educated at Horris Hill preparatory school near Newbury, and Winchester College, where he won a scholarship. Archie left school in 1914, and two years later, he joined the Royal Field Artillery of the 51st Highland Division as a second lieutenant. His experiences fighting on the Western Front were to have a great influence on the rest of his life.

The 51st, known by the Germans as the 'Ladies from Hell' on account of their kilts, were a renowned force, boasting engagements at Beaumont-Hamel, Arras, and Cambrai. But by the time of the 1918 Spring Offensives, the division was war-worn and under strength; it suffered heavily and Archie Macdonell was invalided back to England, diagnosed with shell shock.

After the war, Macdonell worked with the Friends' Emergency and War Victims Relief Committee, a Quaker mission, on reconstruction in eastern Poland and famine in Russia. Between 1922 and 1927 he was on the headquarters staff of the League of Nations Union, which has prominent mention in *Flight from a Lady* and *Lords and Masters*. In the meantime he stood unsuccessfully as Liberal candidate for Lincoln in the general elections of 1923 and '24. On 31

August 1926, Macdonell married Mona Sabine Mann, daughter of the artist Harrington Mann and his wife, Florence Sabine Pasley. They had one daughter, Jennifer. It wasn't a happy marriage and they divorced in 1937, Mona citing her husband's adultery.

A. G. Macdonell began his career as an author in 1927 writing detective stories, sometimes under the pseudonyms Neil Gordon or John Cameron. He was also highly regarded at this time as a pugnacious and perceptive drama critic; he frequently contributed to the *London Mercury*, a literary journal founded in 1919 by John Collings Squire, the poet, writer, and journalist, and Archie's close friend.

By 1933 Macdonell had produced nine books, but it was only with the publication in that year of *England, Their England* that he truly established his reputation as an author. A gentle, affectionate satire of eccentric English customs and society, *England, Their England* was highly praised and won the prestigious James Tait Black Award in 1933. Macdonell capitalized on this success with another satire, *How Like an Angel* (1934), which parodied the 'bright young things' and the British legal system. The military history *Napoleon and his Marshals* (1934) signaled a new direction; although Macdonell thought it poorly rewarded financially, the book was admired by military experts, and it illustrated the range of his abilities. Between 1933 and 1941, A. G. Macdonell produced eleven more books, including the superlative *Lords and Masters* (1936), which tore into 1930s upper-class hypocrisy in a gripping and prescient thriller, and *The Autobiography of a Cad* (1939), an hilarious mock-memoir of one Edward Fox-Ingleby, ruthless landowner, unscrupulous politician, and consummate scoundrel.

Although it is often overlooked, *Flight from a Lady*, written in the same year as *The Autobiography of a Cad,* has all the hallmarks of a Macdonell classic – intuitive prose with a sharp satirical edge, offering an unusual perspective into a world toppling towards disaster. It is a perfect demonstration of Macdonell's singular ability to inject terrific humour into plot and characters – a lover on the run with his determined mistress in hot pursuit – within a valuable interpretation of contemporary politics and the shape of things to come.

In 1940 Macdonell married his second wife, Rose Paul-Schiff, a Viennese whose family was connected with the banking firm of Warburg Schiff. His health had been weak since the First World War, and he died suddenly of heart failure in his Oxford home on 16 January 1941, at the age of 45.

A tall, athletic man with a close-cropped moustache, he was remembered as a complex individual, 'delightful … but quarrelsome and choleric' by the writer Alec Waugh, who called him the Purple Scot, and by J. B. Morton, as 'a man of conviction, with a quick wit and enthusiasm and … a sense of compassion for every kind of unhappiness.'

6th April, 1939
In an Aeroplane, Over the Thames

Ha-ha! I've bilked you after all, you silly little girl. I've escaped from you at last and I'm never coming back. To me at this moment the loveliest line in all English poetry is King Lear's "Never, never, never, never, never." I'll never see your cold blue eyes again. I'll never tremble again when I hear your footsteps coming down a passage. I'm through. It's all finished. Good-bye, you little donkey.

You never thought I could do it, did you? It never entered your lovely head that any of your captives could slip off the chain. Give them a kiss from me — the poor devils. After all you'll have an extra kiss, once in every three weeks, available for distribution. Give them my meagre share of the bones. Good Heavens! to think that I managed to exist for so long on that occasional, miserable bone. No. That's an injustice. I can afford to be fair now. When the bone did come it was not miserable. It was heaven. It was ecstasy. It was like Flecker's stars, "with few but with how splendid stars."

I won't be seeing those stars again, thank God. So far as I'm concerned, my precious, you're a total and perpetual eclipse, you who once were my sun and moon and all the celestial firmament on high. Here I am, writing this on my knee five thousand feet above the Thames. It's my first flight — my first and, even if I fly every day for the rest of my life, always incomparably my greatest. Flight into freedom! That's what I'm making. Flight into a new life.

The engines are purring away like huge, contented cats, and the sun is lighting up the long, silvery sheet of the wing, and the Steward has just brought me a glass of beer, and at any moment I shall be bursting into a triumphal song. King David had very much the same idea, only he limited himself to the comparatively modest scrutiny of the hills. I've lifted up mine eyes to the heavens. But we both have the same idea about singing. It is the moment for song — something loud and cheerful, built on Wagnerian lines for volume and on Harlem-negroid lines for general style.

It is the moment for a modern swing version of the *Te Deum*. Battle was joined against overwhelming odds, and victory has been snatched from an ice-blue, golden-haired, silver-voiced harpy who had never been defeated before.

Have with you, David, my bold. Twang the lyre, clash the cymbals, polish up the sackbut and tune the psaltery, and get ready with me to dance before the Ark of the Covenant. "We are the boys who make a noise when the thundering cannons roar," as Nigel Playfair used to sing.

The skies are bright, my heart is full of joy and excitement, and not even the filthy housingschemes of suburban London can depress me. We are passing over one of them now. They are pretty poisonous as seen from the ground. From the air they are slabs of fungus, eating into the parks and meadows of rural England. But what do I care?

I'm not going to live in one of their revolting little plaster boxes, and I'm never going to see them again, or rural England, or St. James's Street, or you, or anything else out of the past. It is finished.

The housing-scheme has vanished under the aeroplane, and its place has been taken by Tilbury docks. Two half-inch liners — pure white — are moored in them, One of them must be the P & O I originally meant to escape in. Thank goodness I changed my mind. Creeping along at eighteen or twenty miles an hour would have been intolerable, with a radiogram from you dropping in every hour or two, insulting, bullying, wheedling, lachrymose, pathetic, in turns or all at once. But here, in this glorious machine, at two hundred miles an hour, I am safe even from your long, velvety paw, Pussy-Cat.

I honestly believe that if I'd gone by P. & O., you'd have flown to Marseilles to try to fetch me back. I remember you once said to me, in the Savoy Grill, "I never let my men go." Well, I've gone, without so much as a by-your-leave, or a kiss-your-hand.

You never let your men go, huh? What divine arrogance! What superb self-confidence! What — in short — sauce!

Let this be a lesson to you, you beautiful latter-day bashi-bazouk, not to assume that every man is a fool for ever. Lincoln had something to say on the subject, and if you could read words of more than one syllable I'd recommend you to take a glance at what he said. Get your gossipwriter pal to ask the library of his snappy little sheet to type it out for you in capital letters, double-spacing. Then hang it above your bed, and yourself too, if you like.

We're climbing higher and higher. The sun is behind us and there is a faint mist in front. It is going to be a perfect evening — my first of freedom for many a long year. It is a blessed feeling. The French knew a thing or two when they pushed over the Bastille. And don't run away with the idea that there may turn out only to have been a prisoner inside it who didn't want to get out. This one has pushed over his own Bastille, and he's "for off " as the Scots say, at two hundred miles an hour.

No, my pet, you'll have to think up a better alibi than that, to cover your first defeat. I wonder what exactly you are going to say to the world. You'll have to say something. You had paraded me pretty flauntingly, hadn't you? You can't suddenly stop, without a word of explanation. You can't take the chain-gang out into the Park of a Sunday morning with such a very conspicuous gap in it, and have no answer ready.

But you won't have to start on that face-saving problem until to-morrow morning, when this letter reaches you. I will send you some suggestions in my next letter which may be helpful. Or indeed they may not. But as I don't care two straws whether that lovely little face of yours is saved or not, it's all one to Dandy as Sir Walter's Immortal used to say. And now the coast of Holland is ahead of us, so I'll stop.

Good-bye, lady. Have a nice time. I bet it won't be half as nice as the time I'm going to have.

None of my love to you. R.

P.S. — You silly little girl.

P.P.S. — It occurs to me that Lincoln's famous crack was made all in words of one syllable. I'd forgotten that he was addressing the American nation. So you'll be able to understand it after all — or at any rate bits of it.

6th April, 1939
The Hague

I am writing this the same evening to give you a friendly piece of advice — which, considering all the circumstances, is extremely kind of me. It is this. Don't waste your time and money coming over here tomorrow morning and combing the hotels for me. At the very crack of dawn I start; for the East. And don't get hold of a list of hotels, along the regular route of the Dutch Airways to the Far East, because I am chartering a 'plane of my own and I'm going to dodge about just wherever I like.

In fact, poor darling, pursuit is impossible even for a girl of your tenacity and octopus-like grip. I have made all arrangements to cover my tracks.

My plans have been maturing for some while, under that dainty nose, than the end of which you could see no further. Nothing has been left to chance. Trusty friends smuggled maps into my cell, hidden in loaves and cakes; they sent me a file for the prison-bars; a silk rope arrived in a gingerbread; a compass in a smoking dish of tripe; a false moustache was concealed in a lobster armoricaine and only needed to be thoroughly cleaned. Skeleton keys, dried soups, solidified alcohol, primus stoves, chocolate, and every known ingredient to a successful get-away was provided for me by my stout allies.

Not least among them is my aeroplane. (You have a friend who has devoted a lifetime to persuading the British public to call it "airplane." But then he also thought he could persuade the British public to imagine that the British Isles are situated somewhere near the Bermudas, or at any rate could be taken there if a war seemed imminent.)

As I was saying, not least is my aeroplane, smuggled into my dungeon between the leaves of a cheque-book, like a dried fern.

What I mean is, O slow-minded Pussy, that I heard a rumour that the Dutch hired out aeroplanes to private citizens who wanted to charter them, and this is just what I have done. I have my own machine and my own crew, and I can make my own course.

Sold again, Velvet Paw. And if you are thinking of taking your claws to that cats'-parlour in Dover Street for a nice little bit of sharpening, again you would be wasting time and money. They are quite sharp enough already for the pathetic little fool-mice who creep round you. And no amount of sharpening will help you to catch the grand Flying Mouse in his charter-aeroplane.

I had a glimpse of Holland between the sea and the airport at Amsterdam — incredibly neat little rectangles of agricultural land and irrigation canals everywhere. Made a dash to the Hague to see the pictures in the Mauritshuis — especially the Ver Meer's "View of Delft." I would sooner own it than any other picture I've ever seen.

The Hague is full of people on bicycles — almost as many as in Copenhagen — and has very few beautiful girls, which is an altogether admirable feature. Beautiful girls are only a pest. They do no good to anyone, and they seem to think that they have achieved something of great credit to themselves in being beautiful, and that they unendingly deserve applause for a meritorious act.

God gave them beauty. What they ought to do is to thank God on their knees for it, morning and night, and keep it reasonably clean with soap, water, and scrubbing-brushes. Instead of that, they congratulate God for his good sense; they congratulate the world on being allowed to worship such beauty, and they tinge themselves incessantly with cosmetics.

Pah! If you have to give me a girl at all – which is quite unnecessary anyway because I don't want one — give me a homely damsel with a face like a bit of bread-and-margarine and a homely broad beam, and a grin like a slice of water-melon, and woollen stockings, and a good seat on a push-bicycle, and you can have your Helens and your Montespans and your Phrynes.

It is getting dark. At this moment you will be sitting down to dinner with some poor wretch. His only bit of luck is that you will infallibly have been three-quarters of an hour late, and by so much his doom will have been postponed.

But he won't appreciate it. Pitiful ass. And you'll hypnotize him, with a sad little warmth and mistiness turned on now in those large eyes, as a fire-hydrant is turned on by the expert engineer in charge, and you'll say huskily, "I do hope you haven't been waiting long," and he'll wilt like an asparagus-stick and say, "Oh no, only a few minutes," and then your eyes will become like manganese-hardened, high-speed steel under a cloudless sky and you'll say, "In that case, why were you late?" and he'll protest that, so far from being late, he was a quarter of an hour ahead of time, and you'll ask him why then does he tell silly lies, and another of your neat little evenings will swimmingly be under way.

Now that I come to think of it, "neat" is just the adjective which describes you. You have the true artist's economy of effort. In three sentences you will have manoeuvred the luckless youth — or old fool — it makes no difference — into the position when he must either break out into a cold sweat and begin to stammer, or else smack you smartly on the left side of your divinely beautiful face (unless he happens to be left-handed, in which case he will, of course, smack you smartly on the right side of your divinely beautiful face).

To return. Your technique is neat. I wonder if you used to sit at home on long winter evenings, when you were more or less a young girl, and used to work out a programme of verbal moves in the manner of a chess-play. Thus:

You: So-and-so and so forth. (The Feline Gambit.)
Gent.: An unguarded reply.
You: Queen to Queen's sixth (typically jumping second, third, fourth, and fifth).
Gent.: (bewildered). But you said just now —
You: Queen takes Rook, Bishop, Knight, eleven pawns, and check.
Gent.: (Breaks into undignified perspiration, and his collar and he wilts.)

You then sweep the pieces on to the floor and, while he is picking them up, you have found yet another man to despise in your black, secret little heart.

Just think of the difference between him and me.

He is sweating like a schoolboy in the Ritz or wherever it is, in front of the most beautiful and deadly thing that God has created for quite a while — including the latest specimen of Deadly Nightshade — whereas I am sitting cool, calm, collected, and wonderfully indifferent, in front of the entire female population of the Hague, who are dashing backwards and forwards on bicycles.

No one admires more than I do, in theory, the general curves of the female posterior, and although they are not set off to the best advantage by the saddle of the bicycle, nor by the physical attitude which, apparently, bicycling demands of its devotees, nevertheless it is vastly preferable to the chess-game as invented by you and played by you in the grill-rooms of London.

So give me the bicycle and the woollen stockings every time. And you keep your pitiful asses. And with that, and with the memory of heavenly beauty in my mind — no, not you, dear, this time. The Ver Meer — I am going to bed.

Good night. I, about to live, salute you, indifferently. R.

P.S. — Poor small chiquitita. (Spanish. Get one of the Argentine platoon to interpret for you. Or, if the Argentine boys have gone to Deauville, the Chilean squad will oblige, I am sure. Will be only too glad to oblige in any way. Won't they? Yes?)

APPENDIX

A few Suggestions for Face-saving

(1) Appear in dead black for a week and announce, tenderly, that poor darling
    R. (*a*) has died of a broken heart or (*b*) has shot himself in Boulogne for

love of you, and that the *Préfet de Police* is hushing the whole thing up, also for love of you.

(2) Say that I've become a monk, in love-sick despair, and will be wearing a dressing-gown for the rest of my life, and manufacturing Green Chartreuse.

(3) Say that I have caught yellow fever in Peru whither you had sent me to find the treasure of the Incas.

(4) Say that I've gone to fetch you a rose from Shiraz and that I'm bringing it back in a refrigerator.

(5) Say that you were bored to death with the sight of me and threw me out. (No one will believe this.)

(6) But don't, my darling snippet, don't on any account tell them the truth and say that I was bored to death with you. (Because everyone will believe this.)

I remain, your obedient servant (which is what I don't do and am not), R.

7th April, 1939. 5.30 A.M.
Just out of Amsterdam

At this moment you are probably going to bed, sleepy, and victorious as ever. I am up — literally up — and wide awake.

Bobby Browning wrote once — in one of his intelligible moments:

Dear pilgrim, art thou for the East indeed?

I wouldn't be so silly as to think for a moment that you are likely to call me anything remotely as kind as "dear pilgrim," but whatever you do call me, by thunder! I am for the East indeed.

Ten thousand miles are going to be put between you and me in a very short time, and here I am — laying the first of them over my shoulder — as Kipling says somewhere — at the rate of three and a half a minute in my terrific charter-'plane.

I left Schipol, the Amsterdam aerodrome, one of the three greatest airports, they tell me, with Tempelhofer and Singapore, in the Eastern hemisphere, in the early morning, a few minutes ago.

It was dull and drab, and I thought for one moment that there was no justice in the world. On an occasion like this, when a hero was setting out on the most triumphant flight that has ever been undertaken by any man, a dull and drab morning was a monstrous blow to one's instinctive (though always rather pathetic) sense of fair play.

The 'plane taxied to the end of the concrete runway, quivered, started forward with a small bounce, ran down the runway, rose gracefully and banked, and as it climbed over Holland, the sun came out over the tulip-fields. And I knew that God, or whatever you like to call it, is on the side of heroes who make Flights from Ladies.

The patchwork quilt was there below us, red, yellow, orange, dark brown, pink, just like the work of long years of stitching that used to come out of English cottages in the days when there really were handicrafts.

We rose over this fantasy of colour and left it behind and are now heading south.

I am sleepy after my early start — we left the hotel at four o'clock in the morning — and so I'm going to have an hour's nap. The main object has been achieved. I am for the East and I will never see you again.

. . . . .

I'm suddenly in a bad temper. We have climbed above a dense canopy of thick, white cloud, and for a couple of hours there's been nothing to do but either look up at a boringly blue sky or down at a boringly white mass of cotton-wool. Nature can be a tedious old party. Rightly is she so often described, by the sort of authors you, my sweet, read and enjoy, as Dame Nature. A D.B.E. is as much as she's worth.

I come from a family which is apt to admire sunsets, in spite of a shock which they once got from Oscar Wilde. He was visiting my grandfather's house on one occasion, and after dinner the party trooped out onto the verandah and found a particularly violent specimen on exhibition. My uncles and aunts instantly took deep breaths in order to gasp with a pretty enthusiasm, when Wilde paralysed them with a gently contemptuous, "what a foolish sky." The family, fortunately, managed to suppress their gasps and substitute scorn and indignation. It took them years to get over the shock. But they did get over it, and now are as warm on a sunset as ever.

Still clouds, nothing as far as the eye can reach, north, south, east, west, nothing except clouds and ourselves.

I am getting angrier every minute — that is to say every three miles. For my Commander assures me that, although we appear to be hardly moving, we're actually doing a hundred and eighty miles an hour. But why should I be doing it at all? That's what I want to know. Why should I have let a snip like you drive me out of England for ever? Just because a ridiculous creature has a pretty face and an unpleasant nature, why should I be cutting all my old ties and going to settle for life in Tahiti or Hawaii or somewhere?

Men are fools.

I would give a lot to be sauntering in the May sunshine up Bond Street at this moment — provided, of course, that there was no chance of meeting you sauntering the other way. That was always the snag. I always longed to meet you, and then I hated it when I did. Do you remember that French song, "*Je tremble quand je vois ton visage*"? Of course you don't. Menu French is all the French that you know, and you have to ask an Italian waiter to translate even that for you.

But what is the sense of trembling when you see someone's face? It is undignified, it is weakminded, and it doesn't get you anywhere with the owner of the face. She only despises you, and turns away to some half-witted oaf who would be far more likely to smack her face than tremble at it.

So here I am, above a lot of blasted clouds, and I'll never see Bond Street again. I won't hear Atkinson's carillon, or dodge quickly past Cartier's with a lady — any lady — tripping along beside me and trying to edge me through those fairy portals, — I can still hear a small, firm voice saying, "Whatever you do, don't give me old paste," — and I'll never again linger in front of Sotheby's.

Hullo, the clouds are thinning. It's too good to be true. I haven't the faintest idea where we are. Yes, they are thinning very quickly. There's a small muddy stream below us, twisting about and full of islands, and now I can see rows of thin, dark trees, and the red roofs of houses, and beside the stream there's a hamlet, red and yellow in the morning sun. And there's an odd sort of pier sticking out from the hamlet half-way across the stream. I never saw an inland pier before. These must be an odd folk.

Half a moment — I *have* seen something like that before. Good Lord! it's Avignon. Here's a grand series of happy omens. The ancients used to take the omens before they set out on a momentous journey, but here am I being handed the omens on a plate. My first glimpse of the sun on my journey comes to me when I am exactly over the bridge where all the world dances, and exactly over the great palace whence those Holy Fathers at last escaped from their captivity. Sun, dancing, and escape. Perfect. I shall come down at Marseilles for lunch and I'll drink a whacking great bottle of Château-Neuf-du-Pape in honour of the Gods who send omens, in honour of the French who make wine and songs, and in honour of the men who built the Château-Neuf. I can still see it faintly, far behind us now. Seen from the air, it dominates the town a great deal more than it does, according to my recollection, seen from the ground.

So the little muddy stream turns out to be the turbulent, tumbling Rhône.

My spirits have gone up prodigiously. What do I care even if you have driven me out of that ludicrous square mile of insincerity and cruelty which lies between the Parks of London's absurdly-labelled "West End"? It isn't West and it isn't an End. You'll still be frittering about from hair-dressers to luncheons, while I'm crossing the seven seas of the world and while I'm exchanging Atkinson's carillon for the silver bells of Atlantis.

Now we are over Cézanne's country, the rocky hillsides of Provence with their dusty, grey-green scrub and their outcrops of whitish stone and their patches of red earth, and away in front of us on the right is the shallow lake of the Étang de Berre with a row of French seaplanes lying on it; and the airport of Marignane.

In five minutes I shall be tackling my bottle of Château-Neuf in the sunshine while you, I have every reason to suppose, will be drinking a nasty little mixture of spirits and the lowest form of Italian wine, on a wet morning, with a cold wind blowing, and talking to a fool with a receding chin, whose conversation consists entirely of malicious gossip about intimate friends whom he calls "Darling " when he meets them. Bah!

Later
Still Marignane

I had to stay at Marignane longer than I intended — three hours in fact. And they were a nerve-racking three hours. For what was more likely than that you would arrive out of the sky at any moment armed with an enchanting smile and a steel lasso, and a set of handcuffs? I was ready to swim the Étang like a sort of inverted Leander. Anything to escape the pursuing Hero. (Why is a famous rowing-club called after the most famous swimmer in history? But you wouldn't know. Nor do I, for that matter.) When you come to think of it, the pursuing Hero, and you, are just like the North West Mounted Police. You never let up when you want to get your man.

The reason for the dangerous delay was that I picked up a copy of *Le Petit Provençal* (a newspaper) and found that the Junior Thug of Europe was on the point of breaking eleven more treaties, thereby bringing his score of broken treaties to sixty-three as against the hundred and twenty-eight of the Senior Partner in Thuggee. Now it so happens that I am planning to cross over part of what is comically called the Italian Empire and to spend tonight actually in an Italian town, so naturally I was a little alarmed at the situation. There was always the possibility, an outside chance certainly, but still a possibility, that the British Government might honour one of its pledges at last and go to the rescue of the State in danger. In which case I might land on Italian soil to find that I had only jumped out of one prison into another, which would be, a sad anti-climax to a Flight to Freedom.

But believe me, Lady, if the worst came to the worst, I would sooner be in the power of the heroes of Caporetto and the warriors of Guadalajara and the immortal conquerors of Abyssinia. One thing is certain. They couldn't harm my soul. And it is my soul that I'm rescuing now. Of the two prisons, theirs must be infinitely preferable to yours. Any prison must be.

So when I got my reply from London — I had radiographed from Marignane to the Foreign Office asking whether I should go on or not — I had no hesitation in going on.

It was only common sense to go on. On the one hand there was the prospect of the lasso and the return to Mayfair. On the other was the chance of an Italian concentration camp. There was really only one possible choice. There would be cruelty in both jails, but at least the organgrinders would give me a little spaghetti and an occasional ice cream, whereas you would only give me a fatal kiss once in three weeks, and then only if you felt kindly disposed.

I forgot to say that the reply from London was to the effect that the day was Whit Monday and so there was no one in the Foreign Office, except some charwomen who were dusting the files of correspondence marked "Urgent," and who were polishing up the Prime Minister's umbrella-stand. The charwomen gave it as their considered opinion by radiogram that there wouldn't be no war, not until Wednesday anyhow, because the Prime Minister had gone away rabbit-shooting and he didn't hold with wars not while he was out rabbit-shooting he didn't, and they advised me in their considered opinion to do just what I bloody well liked, and much they cared.

So I chose the lesser of two evils and I have just started for Naples.

I wish I could have spared the time to dash into Marseilles, but I couldn't risk the pursuit of the Avenging Angel. Marseilles is a fascinating place. It is where they sell a disgusting dish called Bouillabaisse and where the Phœnicians first made a colony in France, and where the British talk Hindustani to the waiters when they land from P. & O. boats on their way — poor, misguided souls-back to England, and where *La Marseillaise* was not written. But it has this to its credit. It was the men of Marseilles who first appreciated that earthquaking song and sang it on their march to Paris in 1792. Belloc has a great passage about it. He is describing the men of Marseilles, and how they "surged up the white deserts along the Rhône, passing the great sheet of vineyards that slopes up the water-shed of Burgundy." And he describes how they sang "an excellent new marching song," and how at last they came to Paris and sang it in even louder voices on the evening of the 30th of June, 1792. They came to the Gates, and the workmen of the southern quarter of Paris joined in the song and called it the *Marseillaise*. Then comes Belloc's immortal paragraph. "No one can describe music; but if in a great space of time the actions of the, French become meaningless and the Revolution ceases to be an origin, someone perhaps will recover this air, as we have recovered a few stray notes of Greek music, and it will carry men back to the Republic."

What were we talking about? It's gone from me. But it doesn't matter. We're now passing that superb *massif*, that great dorsal fin of a grey rock of a mountain which is called Le Mont de La Sainte Victoire. We are flying along its long ridge, and no higher than the Cross upon its highest point. I climbed up to that Cross once, years ago. Or rather, to be honest, I funked the last few yards and stuck at the ruined chapel just below the Cross.

When I came down from the climb I asked a Frenchman, a Provençal, whether they had had Foch or Clemenceau or Poincaré, or who, to dedicate the mountain to the great Victory over the Boche in 1918. He replied with courtesy, but with a certain coolness, that the mountain was so called for the victory which the Roman Consul Marius won over the Teuton barbarians in the year 102 B.C.

We have passed it now, and I can see a silver glimpse of the Durance, and beyond it are the snowy Alps.

Now the Alps themselves are all right. I mean they are high, white, and handsome. But, like so many of the old Dame's productions, they are closely associated with a type of humanity which I dislike. If the Alps only produced gentians and a nice view across the Lake of Geneva on a summer evening, when you're sitting with a girl — no dammit, I didn't mean that and I'd scratch it out only I know you'd take it to the Science Museum to have the words deciphered — anyway, when you're sitting at a pavement-café with nothing important to do except to sip a Dubonnet — then the Alps would be all right.

But it's the winter-sportists who ruin the whole affair. They tie great boards onto their feet and get photographed for the illustrated papers, or else they lie on their stomachs on another sort of board and get photographed for the illustrated papers. Or else they sit in hotel bars and get ditto, ditto.

I am delighted to be able to record that the Alps have now faded into an afternoon mist — not because I wish them any harm, but simply because they suggest velveteen trousers, cut broad . aft, and girlish simpers.

Those are two things I can say for you — and they are just about the only two I can think of just as this moment — you never went to winter-sports and you never simpered. I'll put it on your tombstone — as soon as you like, too — it can't be too soon for me — "She neither ski-d nor simpered."

Hullo, we're out over the Mediterranean now. I can see St. Tropez and St. Maxime, and so farewell to France, the loveliest, greatest, most infuriating, meanest, bravest, most generous, most adorable country in the world. I am sorry I shall never see her again. Her chief fault is that she is too near to Mayfair. So I prefer the Cannibal Islands. There they literally devour men which is so much more honest and straight-forward than Mayfair's method. You put me in mind of Baudelaire's drawing of Jeanne Duval in the paper-covered edition of *Les Fleurs du mal* which I bought at Dunkirk in the days when Long Max was firing at the town from sixteen miles away. She stands with her shoulders thrown back and a dark amused look in her eyes and the smallest of smiles on her lips. She is saying as clearly as any woman ever said it, "You poor fish," and Baudelaire has despairingly scribbled across it, "*Quaerens quem devoret*," which is, as you well know (from your classical education at — where was it?), the Latin for "Seeking whom she may devour."

You may seek me, little one, until those lovely cheeks go as blue as your eyes. You won't find me any more.

It occurs to me that I haven't quite seen the last of France. I have told the Captain of the 'plane to steer over Corsica. We shall be there in a minute or two, so I will stop writing, and concentrate upon sightseeing for a bit. Damn! I wish I hadn't used that word "concentrate." It calls up visions of camps in Italy for the duration of a nasty war. Let's hope Britain won't get a sudden rush of blood to the head today, and substitute War with Honour for her traditional Peace with Honour, before I can put Italy between you and me.

Corsica below. I'll write again.

With a cold glance. R.

P.S. — You missed a big chance at Marignane. Your spies let you down. You ought to sack one or two, or worse punishment still, you ought not to sack one or two.

Later the same night
Naples

Safe so far. Unless war is declared before 6 A.M. tomorrow I shall escape the clutches of the mighty warriors of Caporetto. And surely no British Conservative statesman would ever declare war at night. It would hardly be cricket.

I crept timidly out of the 'plane at the airport, expecting droves of secret police and bayonets and machine-guns. Nothing happened. Vesuvius was quietly steaming away into the evening sky, but Vesuvius was the only sign of activity for quite a while. At last a hero emerged from an office looking exactly as George Robey would look at the Coliseum in a skit on the Austrian Tyrol. He was wearing a dull green uniform which consisted of shapeless plus-fours tucked into puttees that might have been rolled by a drunk recruit, in a hurry, at midnight, without a light; a tunic that would have made a regimental tailor burst into bitter tears; a Sam-Browne belt; and a green felt hat which came down over his ears, and was shaped like a French steel-helmet. Perhaps it really was the Italian substitute for a steel-helmet. Perhaps it was symbolical of the modern Italy. Perhaps their bayonets are made of felt, and their guns, and their characters. Who knows? At the moment only those Republican Spaniards who fought against them at Guadalajara know what the characters of the felt-hatted cards really are like when it comes to the field of battle. And the Spaniards have been mostly murdered by now by the "very great Christian gentleman," General Franco. "Great Christian" my foot.

However this may be, that was the pantaloon-outfit of this tubby little ice cream-ero together with the inevitable revolver in a black holster and a jack-knife in a sheath, reminiscent of boy scouting, but probably only added to make him feel the devil of a fellow who could kick a woman as soon as look at her.

The little tub rolled across the airport like a diffident, apologetic clown, this inheritor of the Legions of Rome. Vesuvius, steaming away indifferently, has looked down upon generations of soldiers ever since the men of Rome came down its way in the days of the Republic, but I doubt if it has ever had occasion for such a volcanic laugh.

Perhaps Ferdinand Bomba's men were the nearest approach. That tyrant, murderer, and stamper-out of freedom, had an occasional bit of humour in his make-up. When his Prime Minister told him that he proposed to change the uniform of the Neapolitan army from blue to green (or *vice versa*, I've forgotten which), Bomba replied engagingly, "Put them in blue, or put them in green. They'll run away just the same."

But the Italians are not like that nowadays. They are terrific fellows. They are so stout-hearted that they can sign treaties of friendship with unarmed black men and then poison them with mustard gas; they are so dashed brave that they can bombard helpless refugees on Corfu and then claim compensation for it. They are, in fact, the Goods. They admit it themselves.

. . .

So I escaped arrest and I'm sitting at my hotel window looking out across the Bay of Naples, wishing that a mist hadn't hung over Sorrento all the evening and that I could write one-tenth as well as Norman Douglas. What a book *South Wind* is! It is one of the great ones of our time. There's wit and wisdom for you. There's a mastery of subtle satire. Evelyn Waugh is the nearest we have to Douglas, though I often think John Collier will beat him in the end if he works hard enough. But Collier is so elusive. And he spends so much time in arguing with country gentry about electric lights; or in dominating Mrs. Patrick Campbell on the floor of a Hollywood studio (and when you remember that Mrs. Patrick Campbell is like a majestic version of the Albert Hall and John Collier is four feet high, you'll admit that this is no mean feat).

All of which high-brow literary criticism comes out of a view of Capri's silhouette against the stars.

Let me see. Where did I finish up my last letter which I posted at the airport? Oh yes. I was just reaching Corsica.

Somehow it did not move me very much. No one knows better than you, *cara mia*, how fascinated I have always been by that rascally little gentleman of Corsica. Have I not bored you with Napoleoniana in half the restaurants of London? But his native island left me cold. At least I have a good precedent. It left him cold too. He landed there, compulsorily, to refill his ships with food and water on the dash back from Egypt in 1799. But he never went back.

So I did not hang about Corsica. Instead I went eastwards to Elba.

I was astonished at its size. It is infinitesimal. It is a thin spit of an island. It is tiny. There are hardly any houses on it, and only the one small town. Yet that man, who had ruled half Europe, sat down with enthusiasm to reorganize his new empire, and to indulge in his lifelong passion — building.

What a nauseating amount of rubbish is talked about Napoleon nowadays. He created his own legend at St. Helena. That has been swept away by historians. But a new legend is being created for him now by knaves and fools, mostly English, and it's going to take the devil of a lot of sweeping away.

The modern version of Napoleon falls under very simple headings.

Firstly: the fellow wasn't a gentleman (Wellington). It was Napoleon who ordered the surgeons to save Marie Louise first, to whom he was indifferent, and afterwards to save the baby boy whom he so passionately wanted; it was Napoleon who said, "Madame, respect the burden"; and it was Wellington who allowed Ney to be shot. This part of the legend is designed to prove that the English are the only real gentlemen, and that Frenchmen never take baths.

Secondly: that Napoleon's only lasting achievement was the Code Napoleon.

This is part of the English Oligarchy's *façade*. If there is one thing that the English Oligarch is ready to die for — no, don't shout at once that it's his country, because it isn't — it's his Privileges. The English aristocrats cling to their Privileges with an even greater tenacity than the girls who frequent picture-palaces cling, in the slightly dubious words of the most brilliant Limerick of our time, cling to — well! don't let's go on about it. The last word is somewhat ambiguous.

But — and here is the point — Napoleon swept away the Privileges of half Europe. He took them by the throat. When they came towards him, dressed in the white coats of Austria, he knocked them down at Marengo. When the Privileges popped up again a few years later, he bounced them in all directions at Austerlitz, and when the Prussian donkeys ventured a fall with him at Jena on behalf of the same beastly cause, they had to bolt so quickly, and so ineffectually, that they hardly had any breath left to bray with.

That was Napoleon's achievement. That he destroyed Privilege in Europe outside England and Russia. And he shook Privilege to its greasy marrow-bones even in those two.

Therefore the legend had to be invented that he only created the Code Napoleon.

What he actually created was the Modern World.

You and I, alabaster poppet, may think that the Modern World is a not very good one. But that is not what I am talking about just now (although I will certainly be talking to you about it in a day or two unless I tumble into the Persian Gulf without a life-belt). The point is that, whatever the Modern World is, good, bad, mediocre, or just plain mud, Napoleon made it.

Thirdly: (so the modern legend runs) that Napoleon was exactly the same as our newspaper proprietors, or any other variety of big businessmen. The chief characteristic of those chaps is to march about the place dismissing

25

subordinates. The idea is that if you sack a few clerks on the spot, therefore you are Napoleonic.

Napoleon's ruin was very largely due to the fact that he refused to sack clerks, captains, generals, and marshals, however often they betrayed him.

But there it is. Fools are fools. And knaves are knaves. And the English legend about Napoleon is a mixture of knavery and folly. With a vast deal of ignorance thrown in.

Elba is out of sight now. I am glad. It was a sad moment in history. Napoleon was gaily making the best of a bad job, while Metternich was trying to get him poisoned, and the English Oligarchy was straining every nerve to prevent the money going to Elba which had been guaranteed by the English Oligarchy under the Treaty.

But after all, what is a Guarantee when it is given by the English Oligarchy? Ask Czechoslovakia. They will tell you all about those jolly Guarantees.

And who am I to blame the English for failing to carry out their obligations? I am only sitting here in this hotel because of that failure. There are parts of the world in which they say that an Englishman's word is as good as his bond. Just as good, they add.

But I'm wandering. Let us come back to the subject. Which was, of course, your exquisite navy-blue eyes. At least I think it was.

Who are they shining on now, I wonder? God help him and succour him through the dread times ahead of him, whoever he is. Poor swob.

Napoleon had his troubles too, especially when he rode off to the immortal campaign of '96 and left Josephine behind in Paris. But he got over them all right, like all stout men and true, and he lived to make the only really intelligent remark about women that has ever been made, about the occupation of the idle man and the recreation of the warrior. And the moment he had come to that conclusion, a woman at once fell in love with him.

Do you suppose Walewska would have given him another thought, except as the conqueror of Austerlitz, if he had still been the passionate adorer of women that he was in '96? She would not. She would have gone to bed with him, just to annoy her girlfriends and to have something to boast about over the drawing-room tea in the high society of Warsaw. But she would never have fallen in love with him.

Which only shows what women are.

Shakespeare knew all about it. He knew everything about everything. And nobody has ever noticed until this very moment that he made a symbolical gesture of his ultimate feelings about women when he bequeathed to one of you, in his will, his "second-best bed."

As he was supreme in all else, so he was supreme in insult. It is the world's record in insults to women.

Where was I? Oh yes, rambling on about the conqueror of Austerlitz. And that's another strange business about Napoleon. The British have combined to spread the legend that he is the world's Number One soldier. He is nothing of the kind. He threw away five separate magnificent armies. The first was in Egypt where his men, whom he abandoned, were only saved by diplomatic manoeuvring; the second was in Spain; the third was in Russia; the fourth was at Leipzig; and the fifth, and incomparably the best, was at Waterloo.

Look at our own Marlborough. Not once did he put a foot wrong in the whole of his long and intricate campaigns.

But the English don't like him. He was too brilliant. So the nation (which afterwards thought that Haig was a general!) discarded Marlborough, and has continued to discard him, and put Napoleon on the supreme pedestal. Besides, we beat Napoleon, and so the higher the pedestal the higher the English.

After Elba we cruised along the Italian coast and passed over the reclamation land where the Pontine Marshes used to be. To give the devil a little of his due (and how I would love to give him his whole due), he has certainly made a job of the reclamation. Where there used to be only dismal marshes, breeding malaria and doing no good to anyone, there are now neat little farms looking almost like Holland from the air. The roads are mathematically perfect, and the little houses with red roofs are beautifully spaced along the roads. At the back of each house is a rectangle of farmland.

Littoria itself is the town which Mussolini has created in the middle of it all. It's purely artificial, of course, but it is done so infinitely better than the monstrous growths in England. In the Pontine Marshes one single mind has been at work, and the result is perfect coordination. In England ten thousand fools are allowed to build what they like where they like and how they like, and the result is pieces of fun like the Kingston Bypass and the Great West Road.

I don't hold with Benito, as I think even you will have gathered by this time, but his new country, seen from the air, is really rather impressive. And I confess it with profound reluctance, thereby showing the essential nobility of my character.

We crossed the mouth of the Tiber, and I could see the smoke of Rome rising in the distance. In normal times I would have swung leftwards and had a glance at the Eternal City, but politics are politics and I have seen fearsome accounts of Italian anti-aircraft artillery. I felt that they might easily take a pop at a strange aeroplane coming from the direction of England and France, and so I kept my distance.

The Sabine Hills were covered with snow, and a little of my old classics came back to me. But I put them firmly out of my mind. The word "Sabine" conveys the exact opposite of what I am doing at this moment. The Romans went there to do precisely what I am flying to the ends of the world to avoid. And if I start quoting Horace, even to myself, I am bound to arrive in a very short time at:

Dulce ridentem Lalagen amabo,
Dulce loquentem.

You did laugh sweetly. I grant it you. You did talk sweetly. All right, all right, I grant it all to you. And I did love it all. But never no more. What we want are a pack of ravens crying, "Never more."

So let nothing more be said about the Sabine Hills.

In the Gulf of Gaeta warships were moored, so we hastily steered out to sea again to avoid misunderstandings, and it wasn't until they were safely behind us that we crossed over to the mainland and made for Vesuvius.

Certainly the Bay is good. It is very good indeed. Though I think the Neapolitans overstate the case with their "See Naples and die" stuff. A much truer epigram was the one which landed Sir John Squire in such a turmoil of outraged civic pride when he casually wrote, "Die before you see Peacehaven." But all the same I see the Neapolitans' point. The Bay of Naples is undoubtedly in the Sydney-Harbour-Rio-de-Janeiro class.

The Neapolitans themselves are as eternal as their volcano. They never alter for a moment. Gentlemen in faultless evening-dress still accost you in the streets and in the same breath offer to change your money, sell you a bit of faked jewellery, or to provide you with entertainment — "very strange, very curious" — at the biggest hotel on the water-front.

I managed to resist all these temptations, and fought my way through these immaculate gents down to the old castle.

But I soon came away. There were too many little heroes loafing about and giggling, and there were too many memories of Emma, Lady Hamilton. It was in this Bay of Naples that one of the most successful and characteristic of your sex brought off one of her finest coups.

Superficially she did it to please the Queen of Naples who hated her husband's subjects — the ancestors of these greasy little fellows who giggled round me — and always urged him and egged him, as sweet delicate women will do if they get half a chance, to treat them as brutally as possible. As I say, Emma ostensibly worked her grand coup to please this woman. But I don't believe for a moment that that was Emma's real motive. I don't believe any woman would go to such lengths to please another woman. You don't do such things — bless your dear, loving little hearts — not in real life you don't.

No, no, Emma was inspired by the old, old motive, and it's quite a different one and, taken all in all, not so loving-hearted. She had a man in her power, and she wanted to show the world, and even more she wanted to show herself, just how far she could drive him. So she drove Nelson to the murder of a noble and gallant gentleman. More was lost than Caraccioli's life when Nelson's jolly tars — the press-ganged dregs of England's slums — obeyed his orders and strung the Neapolitan patriot up to the yardarm in the Bay of Naples. They obeyed his orders as promptly as Nelson obeyed his. Or rather, as he obeyed them when they came from Emma. Orders from superior officers were a different matter and could be blind-eyed whenever necessary. But Emma had more power than the Lords of the Admiralty, and the greatest of all sailors quartered his ducal and lordly arms with a gallows.

What a fool! But only one of myriads.

Incidentally, what a curious effect Nelson has had upon the English character, both ashore and at sea. If ever a sailor planned out his strategy and his tactics, it was Nelson. Every imaginable contingency was worked out on paper long before the enemy fleet was sighted. He would summon his captains from their battleships night after night to his cabin in the flagship, and laboriously go over and over the various situations which they might be faced with when at last the watch shouted "Sail ahead," or whatever it is that nautical sentinels shout.

"If we find the damned scoundrels" — for that was how Nelson usually referred to his opponents — "in such and such a position, we will do so-and-so. If on the other hand the position of the damned scoundrels is this-and-that, etc. etc. etc."

But all this meticulous preparation, and all this devotion to technical efficiency, has been either forgotten or rather sheepishly shoved aside as un-English. Nowadays the "Nelson touch" means nothing else but speed and courage. It no longer matters what an Admiral or a financier or a newspaper-proprietor does, so long as he does it without hesitation or apparent fear. In fact, the less he thinks, and the more he resembles a bull at a gate, the nearer he is to the famous "touch." The classic case is Admiral Beatty at Jutland.

The magnificent way in which Beatty thundered into action with his battle-cruisers seized the imagination of public and politician, and, on the strength of that thrilling dash across the North Sea, his lordship in life was bounced up the ladder into the Supreme Command, and after death is to be tugged in effigy into Trafalgar Square, although his strategy, his tactics, his gunnery, his navigation, his signalling, and his co-operation, have since been proved, all of them, to have been indifferent.

Whereas Jellicoe — oh! well, let's leave it. A fat lot you care about naval history. So long as there are plenty of pretty gentlemen ready to die for you, you don't mind how they die or when or where. But have you ever made a man commit murder for you? Have you ever ordered the assassination of a noble and gallant gentleman? If you haven't, then Emma is one up on you. Fancy being outdone by a woman of forty-five who looked a washerwoman. I'm ashamed of you. Why not despatch one of your adorers to despatch me? I would fill the bill.

The lights are faintly visible over at Castellamare and the air is laden with the fragrance of soldier-chewed garlic. The Duce has boasted about the terror which his eight million bayonets are ready to strike into democratic hearts. He'd do more with eight million sticks of that revolting vegetable.

I'm going to turn in now. Tomorrow I'm off again, but not to Alexandria, as you might think. I'm taking no chances. Alexandria is the next routine-station on the Dutch Airways line, and I am going to get off that line at once. You might intercept me somehow. I don't trust you an inch, my pretty one.

Ex-yours, R.

P.S. — Miaow.

8th April, 1939
Over the Mediterranean

I'm off on a very tricky journey. There's been nothing to compare with it since Mr. Masefield's Reynard spent a hundred and twenty-three pages of rhymes, and about a couple of dozen pages out of local guide-books, in dodging Mr. Masefield's fox-dogs and his crowd of fox-hunters.

> The sound of the nearness sent a flood
> Of terror of death through the fox's blood.
> He upped his brush and he cocked his nose,
> And he went upwind as a racer goes.

But there's one thing in common between me and Reynard (besides a couple of gallant souls) and that is that we both escaped.

He and I are both of us pretty foxy, thank you. Here I am loping along — not too fast, not too slowly, not in a panic, but not in any blind carelessness, full of confidence, but wary enough to twist and turn just in case the Hound of Hell puts on an unexpected turn of speed or, more likely, brilliantly cuts off a corner.

For this I will say of you, you cut a corner more finely and more surely than any human being I've ever known. And speaking as a fox, it is the quality in a hound that I most dislike. I can jump from A to D more readily than most foxy people; what disconcerts me is when you jump from A to G with a sort of negligence that is as infuriating as the jump itself is frightening. Reynard and I feel rather strongly about this.

Though I'm not frightened now. I've planned this Flight much too carefully for the Lady to catch up. You may stop some of the earths, but you can't stop them all. But it's just as well to understand the devilry of which the Hounds of Hell are capable.

At the moment I am out over the Mediterranean again. There were low, swirling clouds over the Bay of Amalfi, and as they swirled, so the colour of the water changed from the dark greys through all the light greys to the dark, angry blues. It was like the iron shield of a Homeric captain — if they had iron shields, which I very much doubt — but anyway, if they had, and if their batman had been slack in his polishing, their shields would have looked just like the Bay of Amalfi, very smooth, and very dirty, with splashes of iron-blue metal showing through here and there.

Now I am heading south, leaving on my left hand Salerno — where Pope Gregory the Seventh, greatest of all the Mediaeval Popes, lies buried under a red porphyry tomb with no inscription and no effigy and no single mark to tell of the man whose dust is there — and in a few minutes we shall be passing one of the hateful places of Europe.

Yes, I can see Stromboli already. Not that Stromboli is hateful. Far from it. It is superb. But soon we shall see the Lipari Islands — the forgotten prison.

I'll tell you the story of Lipari.

There was a time, years ago, when Signor Mussolini was steadily increasing in power at home and steadily mounting in the raving adulation of all the Kensingtons of all the upper-middleclasses in England.

In Italy he was successfully inventing the legend that he had saved the country from the Red Menace (and adding to that legend the two fairy-tales (i) that he had fought heroically in the World War and (ii) that he had led the march of the Blackshirts on Rome); and in the English Kensingtons — which include the Cheltenhams, the Malverns, the Baths, the Conservative Associations, the City of London, and all the Sillies of the land — he was being worshipped as the man who made the trains of Italy run punctually.

But he had to consolidate his position both in the hearts of his countrymen and in the Sargasso Sea. So Matteotti was murdered in circumstances of unprintable brutality; on the day after the murder Signor Mussolini personally visited Signora Matteotti and assured her that every step was being taken to discover her missing husband; and all liberal-minded opponents of the regime were shipped off to the convict-prisons on the Lipari Islands.

That consolidated his position in Italy.

The position on the Seaweed front was fixed by the official abolition of beggary, the continued running of the express-trains within an hour or two of schedule, and the spread of a new and ingenious story — that Signor Mussolini was the son of a blacksmith (which he is) and a man of astounding virility (which he may be too, for all I know).

This last story was irresistible. The suggestion of blacksmithy strength, both in and out of the smithy, hypnotized the Union of Conservative Women's Associations into a state of adoring sleepiness, and the trick was done.

Matteotti was forgotten. The professors and artists and students and philosophers, who felt that intellectual slavery was a poor exchange for a theoretical train-punctuality, are still in the convict-prisons of these barren, burning warts of lava, and all, all are forgotten by the world. But the Duce is not forgotten. And even the poor jelly-fish who occasionally peer over the waste of seaweed are beginning to wonder. After all, that shiny bald head and that gross, pendulous dewlap are not quite so attractive, even to the Kensingtons, as the story of virility once was. And whereas nobody minded about the Bolshies who were so rightly put in prison, people are beginning to mind quite a bit about the dear Duce's air-force, and sweet Benito's really most un-British way of breaking treaties.

We've passed the Lipari Islands. I'm glad of it. They, and Dachau, and the Fortress of PetroPavlovsk, stink to Heaven with their hellish cruelty and injustice.

There was an exact parallel to our punctual-minded Baldhead's prisons in the days of Bomba. Ferdinand, King, was not much more successful as a soldier than is, or was, Benito, Duce, but he was just as efficient at prison work. And he chose his gaol-birds from the same walks of life. Poerio and Settembrini and Castromediano were gentle and noble idealists, so they, and many others, were sentenced on false evidence to imprisonment in chains for life, on the islands, or in the dungeons of Montefusco.

> Who e'er comes back to life
> From Montefusco's towers
> May boast himself twice born
> Into this world of ours.

Poerio's only comfort in his mildewed, rat-infested cell in Montefusco was the song of a nightingale in the bushes outside, so the gaoler killed the nightingale.

Montefusco — Lipari — Dachau — Petro-Pavlovsk — all are hideous.

I can see in front the magnificent outline of Monte Pellegrino where the Carthaginians encamped under the great Hamilcar somewhere about 250 B.C. and maintained themselves incredibly for three years against all the Sicilian armies of Rome.

And there beyond Pellegrino is the Conca d'Oro, the Shell of Gold, the semicircle of hills round Palermo. I wish I could see the lemons and the oranges, but we're much too high.

Now I am flying across the westernmost corner of Sicily to see three things, and three things only, and I am now coming to the first of them.

It's the little port of Marsala, created by generations of English wine-merchants, and immortalized as the landing-place of Garibaldi.

Just a Mole and a small lighthouse and a row of wine warehouses and the freedom of a country. That's all. Nothing more.

We turn back, eastwards and inwards, to the second of my pilgrimage-places — Calatafimi. It was here that Garibaldi stood under the last terrace which shielded his men from the fire of the Neapolitan troops on the top of the hill — the Pianto dei Greci — and it was here that they asked him in the last desperate hour of the battle, "General, what are we to do?" And he replied, "Italians, here we must die." Then a stone, thrown from above — the two lines of battle were so close, — hit him in the back. It gave him a bit of a shock — quite naturally — but within a couple of seconds he knew what had happened, and he shouted, "Come on. They are throwing stones. Their ammunition is finished," and he led the victorious charge up the hill.

Italy was made there.

I can't distinguish the Pianto from the air. Hills look very much like each other. But I can see the tiny dot, standing all by itself on a wide-open expanse of brown land, which is my third objective. It's the Greek Temple of Segesta. Many of Garibaldi's men — even after a terrible battle in the heat of the day — went three miles out of their line of march to see it. They knew that Freedom is very often the same sort of thing as Beauty. I wonder if they realized that very often also it isn't.

I wish I could land near Castrogiovanni where Pluto behaved so rough to Persephone — I bet she liked it. The combination of wealth, roughness, and hellishness is always irresistible to you girls — but I am afraid of these Italianos. If war is imminent, it would be folly to take a chance. So off again on a new twist, with Mr. Masefield:

> Past Colston's Broom, past Gaunt's, past Shere's,
> Past Foxwhelps' Oasts with their hooded ears,
> Past Monk's Ash Clerewell, past Beggars' Oak,
> Past the great elms blue with the Hinton smoke.

Only I think I go past Etna's smoke instead. I prefer to think of Empedocles rather than British Sportsmen.

Later

We have flown past all the accepted sights of Southern Sicily. Girgenti with its row of dots which I know from past pedestrian tourism to be the honey-yellow temples along the ridge; Syracuse, home of the greatest silver coins of the world and grave of Athenian freedom; Catania with its lemon-groves; Etna, snow-covered, incomparably majestic; Taormina, eddying with Baedekers, translated into all languages; and so past Acireale and out across the Ionian Sea.

I will post this at our next landfall. I don't like you very much. This brings you no good will. R.

P.S. — *O Sole Mio!* Wow!

Same Day
Over the Ionian Sea

Crossing the Ionian Sea I have plenty of time for reflection — nothing being visible except saltwater — and as I have only one subject to reflect about — and I don't want to reflect about it — I have been talking instead to my crew.

These Dutch 'plane-captains are an interesting study. I have flown with one or two of them and I talked to some of them at Amsterdam, and they all have the same fundamental characteristics. They are slow in speech and in action; they are very thoughtful; they are very cheerful; they shoulder responsibility with the utmost readiness if they are certain that they can carry out what they are promising to do; they refuse to accept responsibility if they feel uncertain; and they are incredibly efficient.

The Second Pilot handles the 'plane over the long easy stretches which are more or less routine. But the moment a thunderstorm comes up, or a landing has to be made, the Captain abandons his newspaper, or his nap in the passengers' part of the 'plane, and goes up into the cockpit and takes command. The moment there is even the faintest possibility of trouble, the Captain is on the bridge.

The Captain does all the startings and all the landings. When we are safely packed into the machine in the mornings, and the Wireless-man has got all his weather reports, and the Captain has made certain that the route I want is safe according to the reports, and the Mechanic has satisfied himself that petrol and oil and engines are all in order, and the Steward has loaded his huge thermos-flasks of tea, coffee, and iced water, and has taken a last look at his pocket-book to see that he hasn't left the passports behind, and, most important of everything, it is generally agreed that I, the patron, am comfortably settled into my seat, then the Captain takes charge.

The engines start and run fast and smoothly — the Mechanic has been up since dawn warming them up — and the Captain taxies down slowly to the furthest end of the aerodrome that faces the morning's wind. Then he wheels round into the wind. Then the engines roar more and more loudly and the whole machine quivers until the crucial moment arrives. The 'plane seems to gather itself and sit back on its hind-legs for an instant — just like a horse setting out at a fence — and then it leaps forward down the run-way. It bounces and jolts on the irregularities of the ground until suddenly you realize that it isn't bouncing or jolting any more. You look down and the houses and trees are dropping away beneath you. The nose of the 'plane is tilted and another flight has begun. Half-an-hour later the Captain comes out of the cockpit and studies his maps or a Dutch newspaper. The craftsman's work has been done, once again perfectly, and the Second Pilot can take on.

Meanwhile the Steward brings me some beer and talks.

As we fly over the Ionian Sea, I am enchanted that my Steward begins to talk on the most exactly correct subject he could have hit upon. If he had tried for hours to find a subject more likely to please the Young Master, he could not have made a better job of it.

For, after a few observations about tulips and the size of London and the possible imminence of war, he switched off on to what was obviously his favourite topic — the Dutch struggle for Independence against the Spaniard.

Could anything have been more *à-propos*? Independence, Freedom, that was his theme song, and we would have fallen on each other's necks in a fraternal embrace except for two insuperable objections — firstly, that Young Masters don't go about the place embracing their stewards, and secondly, that fraternal osculation has never been much in my line. In the dear, dead days, gone for ever, thank God, if I had to kiss anyone, it was always a girl, which, of course, has saved me from one sort of ruin to plunge me into another. At least it would have plunged me into another if I hadn't been brave enough to fight my way out, as I am doing now.

So instead of actual fraternization we arrived at a nice compromise. The Steward, a charming lad of about twenty-five in a smart Eton suit of dark blue, rambled on with deep enthusiasm about Leyden and Haarlem and the cutting of dykes and the Sea-Beggars and William of Orange, while I listened to him with both ears and thought of you with the rest of my faculties.

There really isn't very much difference between you and Torquemada. Motley records how the Netherlanders went, at first, like sheep to the rack and the pulley. The more docilely they went, the more eagerly Torquemada oiled the wheels. Isn't that an exact parallel?

And then, when the Netherlanders began to resist, and even began to flood their own beloved country on the chance of drowning those cantankerous and perjured Dukes, Alva and Parma, who so hurt and puzzled and indignant as Torquemada and his boss, Philip II?

So with you, little pet. At this moment you'll be sitting in your flat, tearing your hair, your redyellow-amber- bronze- tawny- lemonade (whichever it happens to be at the moment) hair, to think that you are the modern Torquemada — failed

37

B.A. in the torture tripos. It's just too bad. But you and the Dukes, Alva and Parma, made the same mistake. You all went too far.

I wonder if I have hit upon an eternal truth. Women who get a man tied neatly up to the triangle always go too far. Everyone knows that. It is — as the Babu in *Kim* said — "axiomatic."

But male tyrants, when they get a subject nation in the same position, always go too far also.

Is there, then, a psychological connection between all women, and those rare — thank God — male creatures who become Dictators? It had not occurred to me before. Is there a connection? I must think this out. So I will reluctantly interrupt the Steward's fascinating description of the siege of Berg-Op-Zoom in order to do a little abstract consideration of an important human problem.

Later

Still Over the Ionian Sea

The problem I was worrying about turns out to be quite simple. All women want to be dictators, even if it's only over a weedy little chap with tin-rimmed glasses and a pigeon-chest, and two pound twelve-and-six a week, after fourteen years' service, in an Insurance office, but they only want it because they know that ninety-nine times out of a hundred the weedy little chap will dictate over them if they don't look out. They want to dictate; they don't expect to succeed; and when they do, the blood goes to their heads. So it is with these blackguardly crooks.

They start forlornly as house-painters, or bad journalists, or factory agitators, or generals who have broken their oaths, and they hope for the best. A lucky break comes their way and they are astonished — just like you girls — to find they've got a good nation down.

And they treat the good nation just as you treat the good man.

And ultimately the nation turns — if it is like the Dutch, brave and proud and honourable — and ultimately the man turns if he is like me — well, I hardly like to put in the corresponding adjectives — against the oppressor.

And — here is another axiom — if the Dutch worm or the masculine worm turns against the oppressor with real, rugged, inflexible, determination, then the battle is won.

You will say, with that horrid tip-tilt of the left side- of your small mouth, that neither worms nor men can be rugged. Don't you believe it, little angel. You aren't right all the time. And how I have hated that scornful tip-tilt of your mouth. It was always the left side of it, because the left side is just a thread longer than the right, and so it tilts more easily, and well you know it. And well you know everything about yourself, from your demoniac soul to the millimetrical measurement of your curved lips, so lovely, and so detestable, and (long years ago) so infinitely desirable.

Don't sneer. It was long years ago. In all the time we were together, every minute was an hour, and so on, and so on.

But when I think of those days we spent — where was it — on the Downs, or in the woods of Buckinghamshire, or under the sea-wall at Brighton — the long years seem to be minutes again and yesteryear becomes yesterday. So I won't think of those days. I flatly refuse to think of them.

I want the old happy moments to be as far away as possible. Why should they crowd in upon me? Why should they jostle my new gay thoughts when they are not wanted?

If anything lovely ever happened to me in my life — and I won't admit point-blank that anything lovely ever has — it was a very long time ago, and I've forgotten all about it. Do you hear? Can you read? I've forgotten all about it, I tell you. Damn you.

And let me tell you another thing. In this aeroplane, which I have hired at such enormous expense from the Hollanders, I have not brought my ancestral sun-dial.

"Why?" you may ask. But whether you ask or not — and I can see the graceful yawn — I'm going to tell you. Because sun-dials traditionally mark only the sunny hours. "*Horas non numero nisi serenas.*" And there are no sunny hours between you and me that I want marked. And anyway the Captain of the 'plane wouldn't have taken a sun-dial.

So let the Captain, and our memories, keep all fragrance away. I don't want it, and you wouldn't recognize it, even if you sniffed it with that dainty nose.

It's a funny thing about your nose. It has a poise about it, a sort of subtle elegance, not supercilious in the least, not aristocratic, not plebeian, not challenging, not humble, but just gently confident in its own perfection. How few noses are perfect. How few are anything but monstrosities, like the wart-hog or the gnarled roots of the mangrove. But yours — God help me — is perfect. Many a time I would like to have given it a sharp bopp (as Damon Runyan would say), but always I was dissuaded by its beauty.

But join me on this aerial cruise, my poppet; just you join me on this cruise, uninvited, and you will get an almighty bopp on the noggin.

So don't tell me I didn't warn you.

And now we return to where we were. The Dictators are feminine. They find themselves in power, and they exploit their power ruthlessly.

Good-bye, Dictators. And good-bye, girls. I'm free. I'm singing a song to myself — quietly —— so as not to worry the Steward. It's Basil Hallam's old song, which he sang as he went off to the wars from which he never returned, "Goodbye, girls, I'm through."

The Ionian Sea is still very blue, and I can see land in front of us. So skilful a navigator am I, and so expert is my Captain in following out my general instructions, that I know exactly where I am. As a matter of fact my Captain tells me where I am, and he is always right.

From this point you don't have to read any more because anyway you won't understand a word of what I am talking about, and I am writing entirely for my own amusement. Now that I come to think of it, when I am reading my own writing or when I am listening to myself talking aloud are almost the only times when I do get any amusement. Do you remember what Monsieur Briand, that Peter Pan, and man of the world, and wizard in politics and words (but very bad golfer), said when someone asked him, "Monsieur Briand, why do you talk aloud to yourself so much?" The old Frenchman instantly replied, "It's the only time I am certain of getting an intelligent answer." And that's what I feel at the moment. Anyway, not to put too fine a point upon it — whatever that means — I am now exactly over the Island of Ithaca. It is the first time that I have ever seen Greek soil.

We circle round and round the little island while I think up all kinds of deep and philosophical ideas about how so small a patch of land could have inspired so great a flood of poetry, which is, of course, nonsense. Ithaca, though it's only a blob in the Ionian Sea, is much larger than Stratford-on-Avon. Homer could have produced his stuff out of a dustbin. All the same, it is exciting to look down upon the island of Odysseus, that crafty and dishonest gentleman, using the word "gentleman" in the broadest and most tolerant sense.

Now we are steering for the entrance of the Gulf of Corinth, and I can see the glittering sand which Achelous, the son of Ocean, has poured down for centuries into the sea. There are little islands at the mouth of the river. They used to be different long ago, probably even more decorative and certainly more dangerous, because once upon a time they were nymphs. Achelous in a fit of temper changed them into islands, and I think he was absolutely right.

But think what a pull a chap has if he is a son of Ocean. Picture our own case. We are sitting in my club — as we have sat a hundred times — and I am getting more and more irritated with you and your tantrums and your ingenious ways of annoying, and then you go an inch too far as say, "Oceanovitch, you are nothing but a little baby," and I turn you into the Isle of Wight or something.

Of course there's trouble with the Club Committee for a while, and the BBC. announces an S. O. S. for information about "missing, a girl, five feet ten, blue eyes, golden hair, tip-tilted nose, has sometimes been described as moderately good-looking, talks too much, flashily dressed, last seen in the company of an extraordinarily handsome man of noble carriage, lofty brow, clear, candid eyes, and the expression of innate goodness coupled with concealed suffering."

My only complaint against Achelous is that he was the representative of all fresh water in Greece, which seems to me a rather poor distinction. Apparently he was proud of it. He comes twisting down very slowly from Mount Pindus, away up in the direction of Dodona where the oak trees were sacred to Zeus.

Pindus is not visible. It is rather misty up north. Talking of Dodona, I wish I could trace a poem which I read long years ago somewhere. I can only remember the first verse, and it runs:

> Oh, what did they do in Dodona?
> What did the Dodonians do?
> I speak as the ignorant owner
> Of oaks not a few.

I would like to follow up this plaintive appeal from the harassed quercologist — a word I have invented at this moment to describe a student of oak trees.

What a lot of nymphs there must have been — there are dozens of islands in the delta of the river — and what a wretched life Achelous must have led before he hit upon the happy dodge. Half a dozen nymphs at a time is quite enough for any man.

And now we are coming to one of the most important places in the world — Missolonghi. There is practically nothing to see, but think of the memories which it conjures up to men who are escaping to freedom.

If ever another man was compelled to make a flight from ladies it was poor Byron. Why do you all persecute us so? Why can't you be content with fat columnists, and aged financiers, and seedy foreign gentlemen with fancy titles, and dirty politicians whose necks and whose principles are of an identical dusky hue, and monkey-faced actors, and Orstrylian wool cards from Stinking Sheep Gulch, without that you needs must have a dash at us poor poets as well?

All we ask is to be let alone. But will you do it? No fear. Every woman is Lady Caroline Lamb when a poet is about the place. Volcanoes in porcelain, to adapt George Meredith's phrase. Earthquakes in satin.

Byron made his Flight even more symbolical than mine, because he linked his own freedom with the freedom of Greece. But the idea is the same. He got away. He laid the corner-stone of the independence of Hellas, and I haven't the smallest doubt that for him the least important part of the whole affair was his own death.

So Missolonghi is one of the key pilgrimage shrines of all poets who prefer freedom to the Lady Carolines of this miserable world.

And now we fly straight into compact history. It is a heavenly spring afternoon and the Gulf is so blue that it would be absurd to hunt about for poetical comparisons. All I can say is that it is a real, genuine, honest blue, bright and simple, and quite different from the misty, treacherous blue of those eyes of yours. The Gulf of Corinth on a spring morning is straight-forward and sincere in its shining blueness.

I've got a map on my knees, and the great names are rolling past me — Naupactus, and Locris, and Achaea, and Parnassus, snow-crowned on the right, and then Mount Helicon hiding Thebes, and Plataea, and Leuctra, where Epaminondas smashed those filthy Spartans. I would like to make a pilgrimage to Leuctra one day, to pay my tribute to those heroes who stood up against ruthless, soul-less, organized Nazism.

That is what the Spartans were. Nazis. Brutality, militarism, illiteracy, cruelty, mass-destruction of beauty, swamping of freedom by floods of armed and disciplined men, that was Sparta, and Prussia, and the Third Reich of Herr Hitler.

Did ever a great poem come out of any of the three, or a great picture, or a great preacher, or a great actor, sculptor, philosopher, courtesan, wit, humanitarian, or queen? But Sparta came down from the north and blanketed the land of Homer and Agamemnon and Theseus with a black blanket of hellish barbarism for centuries, and when Athens rose to the nearest point that the human soul has ever reached towards the Pleiades, it was Sparta, with its goose-step and its "Heil, Agesilaus," that beat her down.

Must the goose-step for ever trample on the philosopher? I wonder. Or is the modern Athens, the city of our dreams — dear city of Cecrops, as the poet said, and "shall we not say Dear City of God" with Marcus Aurelius — going to survive by a freak coincidence?

Make no mistake, my pretty one, Athens to-day is facing Sparta, just as she did at Marathon, at Aegospotami, at Chalons, at Tours, at Rhodes and Malta and Lepanto, at Vienna when Sobieski came down with a storm of Catholic horsemen and saved Magdalen Tower from becoming a minaret and Cardinal Manning from being a muezzin, and on the Marne and the Aisne and the Hindenburg Line.

It is the old tale of Light against Darkness. And if we save ourselves, as I think we will, it will be because Sparta is at long last facing a combination which it cannot understand — a race of strange but inflexible realists who are magnificent soldiers, allied to a race of strange but inflexible illusionists who are magnificent sailors. It is pure fluke. But it has happened, and Sparta must face it. The Powers of Darkness do not always win.

But I wish I could see Leuctra. I've seen the Marne.

We are swinging south a little — I want to pass over Corinth — and the long white wings of the 'plane are tilting in the sunlight. Cithaeron has taken the place of Helicon on the left. The woods climb down to the water's edge. There are no houses. It is sombre, even in the sun. Corinth is hardly there. There is nothing to see except the thin canal which looks like a lead pencil made of silver and the mound of the Acrocorinthus. The Romans made a thorough job of it, years before Caesar, when they destroyed the "Light of All Greece." They were dark-hearted soldiers in those days before Virgil and Horace, and they took the marble city on the isthmus and utterly and completely abolished it for no reason whatsoever. They were Spartans, in fact, and Corinth is to-day practically what it was when Lucius Mummius, Roman Consul, — may his soul rot and fester in hell to all eternity, and even longer — left it in 146 B.C.

So we pull away left-handed from Corinth. It has given us the trireme (that rowing-boat which no one understands to this day, not even the Fellows of All Souls), the currant, the Regency bucks, a style of architecture, an amateur football club, and a tradition of beauty.

But perhaps, on reflection, Corinth deserved what it got. In my little classical dictionary I find it recorded of the Corinthians: "With their wealth they became luxurious and licentious. Thus the worship of Aphrodite prevailed in the city, and in her temples a vast number of courtesans were maintained." A year ago — no — six months ago I would have said "Tut tut." Now I say, "Damned fools." If any one worships Aphrodite he gets what he deserves — except Aphrodite. He gets her, of course, but he deserves something better. And when he has got her, he gradually fades from the strong life that men ought to lead, unhampered by small and graceful and elegant pieces of nonsense, and sinks into the luxuriously futile life of the Corinthians. They worshipped Aphrodite and they fell to ruins.

Serve them right.

And now — and now — the dream of a lifetime is coming true. When I was a child of six, seven, eight, or whatever it was, I was brought up on the Greeks. I learnt the Greek alphabet and used to write postcards in Greek letters to my grandfather. My nursery-games were always "Hector and Achilles," or "Odysseus and the Cyclops." I acted in a play about Nausicaa, under a flowering thorn-tree. I was, in fact, a howling classical prig.

And later on, not even a damnable skill at playing silly British pastimes could entirely deter me from following the fortunes of Alcibiades and Themistocles.

And here it is — the land of my dreams — lying beneath me in a sunlit haze.

Aegina, steeply mountained on the far side and green and fertile on the hither side, is on my right. Aegina is romantic and exciting enough — the island which fought so long and so desperately against Athens. Aegina is a handful of history by itself.

But who can look out of the right-hand side of my aeroplane down at Aegina when the immortal of immortals is on the left?

Poor Aegina. So far as I am concerned she will always remain unchronicled as long as the left-hand windows are clear and unfogged. (If I was coming back, it would be the other way round. But then I'm not coming back. See, sweetie? Not coming back ever.)

So on my right Aegina; and on my left Salamis. Salamis, where Rome and Michael Angelo and Shakespeare were made possible. Salamis, where Aeschylus fought for freedom just as Cervantes fought at Lepanto and Shaw-Stewart at the Dardanelles.

Do you remember Shaw-Stewart's

> Was it so hard, Achilles,
> So very hard to die?
> Thou knowest and I know not,
> So much the happier I.

And the last verse in the same poem:

> I will go back this morning
> From Imbros over the sea.
> Stand in the trench, Achilles,
> Flame-capped, and shout for me.

The Bay of Salamis is spread out beneath me. The "rocky brow," on which the Great King perched while his sailors were destroyed, is a low cliff, and a cluster of houses at the water's edge must be Eleusis. The entrance to the Bay is what we call in motoring language to-day "an S-bend," and it is unbelievably narrow. But it was in this narrow entrance that the battle was fought. Themistocles was a clever man. He knew all about the supreme importance of in-fighting when your opponent in the ring is bigger and stronger and faster than you are, but is not so brave. Themistocles cajoled and bluffed the Persians into fighting in the narrow strait where weight was nothing and morale was everything. On paper the Greeks were mad to let themselves be caught in such a small space; in actual fact a master-psychologist was in control of the situation, and it was only in such a small space that in-fighting was possible. So Themistocles fought, while the Great King watched.

> And ships, by thousands, lay below,
> And men in nations; — all were his!

44

He counted them at break of day —
And when the sun set, where were they?

I think the "ships in thousands" is a bit of an exaggeration. There isn't room in the Strait of Salamis for rowing-boats in thousands. But never mind.

A woman fought at Salamis. Artemisia, Queen of Halicarnassus, brought five ships which were better equipped than any in the fleet except the ships of the Sidonians, and she commanded them herself. She performed what are usually called "prodigies of valour" at Salamis, and although the feat which earned her the applause of her commander-in-chief was not exactly creditable, at least it was in perfect harmony with the characteristics of her, and your, Darling, sex.

For in the heat of the engagement she found her warship heading straight for another ship of her own side. The captain of this allied vessel was striking stout blows for the cause, but had quarrelled with the lady at an earlier stage in the campaign. Without a moment's hesitation Artemisia rammed his ship and sank it with all hands.

Her commander-in-chief observed this dashing feat and, never imagining for a moment — the simple fellow — that Artemisia had done anything else than sink an enemy vessel, applauded her loudly and exclaimed, "My men have become women and my women men."

I need hardly add that the simple fellow was Xerxes, the Persian king, and that the girl was fighting on the side of the barbarians for the suppression of freedom and the enslavement of brave men.

We circle round and round over the scene of the battle and at last reluctantly I gave orders to push on. We sail over the Piraeus and over the Acropolis and past Lycabettus and on to the airport at Decelea.

Perhaps I'll write to you again someday. R.

P.S. — By the time I get to my ultimate destination, you'll be quite a well-educated poppet.

Same Day
Athens

Decelea — the name brought back memories. At first I was puzzled. I stared at the Greek letters over the airport's office, and laboriously translated them out of my old sixth-form days. The words were clear — "Air-harbour Decelea." Then I remembered, and I turned instinctively to see where the hill was. It was there, all right, looking down on the aerodrome, a tall, handsome hill, covered with rocks and olive-trees and, here and there, those sorts of crops that I wouldn't know the names of.

I don't suppose fifty people live to-day on the hill at Decelea. Two thousand years ago that hill destroyed the Athens of Themistocles and Pericles and Pheidias. And so, I've no doubt, you think that the whole affair was very admirable. You and Artemisia — and Baudelaire's girl — "*quaerentes quos devoretis*." Barbarians all.

But Decelea, that ordinary hill, that typically boring bit of Balkan landscape, is not simply a bore. It is an eternal proof that you are right. Brute force, square shoulders, illiteracy, goosestepping — all the things that you adore — found their ultimate home-from-home at Decelea. The Spartans fortified the hill and used it as a base — an all-year-round base — from which to harry Attica.

Before they hit upon the dodge of making a permanent occupation of the hill, they used to invade Attica and drive the farmers off their farms and devastate the countryside in the authentic spirit of Attila's Huns, Kaiser Wilhelm's latter-day brand of the same barbarians, and our own authorities in the second part of the Boer War of 1899-1902. But, in the intervals between the invasions, the Attic farmers used to creep out, and save what they could from the wreckage, and harvest any crops that came to maturing during the off-season for Spartans. But when there was no off season, when your muscular friends were perched on Decelea all the time, that was the beginning of the end of fifth-century Athens. Of course the Spartans did not hit upon the idea for themselves. It was handed to the bone-heads as a free present by the most brilliant Athenian of the age, after the Athenians had slung him out of the city into exile for a crime which they couldn't prove that he'd committed and which he almost certainly hadn't. The

Athenians of the fifth century were really very feminine. They governed most of their actions by guess-work. If the guess turned out to be right, they said quietly, "Well, of course. What else did you expect? That's just our intuition." And if the guess turned out to be wrong, either they said nothing more about it and went on to the next thing, or they accused somebody at random of treachery and gave him a smart punishment.

So much for Decelea, whence bone-heads ruined the greatest intellectual age of all.

The sun was going down before I had satisfied all the officials at the airport that my suitcase contained neither opium nor howitzers nor cinematograph appliances, that I had practically no money, and that I had very seldom suffered from smallpox. Two bright planets shone. over the Spartans' hill, Jupiter and, brighter and more beautiful and more self-assertive, of course, Venus.

I motored from the airport along the valley of the Cephisus, that small stream of olive-woods and reeds and wild-flowers.

Oleanders and bougainvillea were casually scattered among the long grasses and the tall ladies'-lace, and every cottage-garden had its patch of cultivated annuals. We came round a sharp bend in the road upon a very tiny donkey whose two panniers were loaded with sweet-peas.

But all too soon the Cephisus is lost behind the loathsome, dusty, noisy, gimcrack suburbs of northern Athens.

The modern city of Athens is just like any other modern city, except that it is dustier. The dust is hot and it has an astonishing knack of getting into places that can be proved conclusively with all the aids of science to be hermetically sealed. The other chief feature is that the city is fuller of dogs than any other, all of whom bark all night. The Athenian dog is of a lung-power and of an endurance that explains Pheidippides and the Marathon race and the Olympic Games.

For the rest, Athens is a city of swagger, big hotels, nice big public buildings, a park, a fashionable promenade under shady trees, a very large number of guides, both professional and amateur, and, as I say, some pretty awful suburbs.

The moment I got to my hotel, I threw my suitcases into the office, fought my way through the guides, and set out on foot to the Acropolis. Someone had told me that it wasn't easy to find, and naturally I sneered in his face. Not find the Acropolis! You might just as well say that if you get out of the train at the Waverley Station in Edinburgh, you would run a grave risk of missing the Castle.

So I refused all offers of help and walked off in the direction which I knew by instinct must be the right one. And in a moment or two my instinct was justified, for I caught a glimpse of it above and between two high buildings.

But, after getting the exact direction, do you think I could find my way up to it? I could not. I went up little, narrow streets — obviously I had to keep on going up — only to find that they suddenly swung away and went down again. I went up little, narrow streets that came to dead-ends. I tried broader streets and found myself back on the big, modern boulevard that I'd started from.

The sun was steadily sinking all the time and I began to think that just by my obstinacy in refusing to drive up on the big motor-road I was going to miss what I'd longed for since I was at school — a first sight of the Parthenon in a spring-time sunset.

At last I found an alley-way that led straight up to the walls, and I almost ran up it and emerged triumphant at the foot of the rock. But the operative phrase in that sentence is "at the foot of." Many a bold soldier must have found himself in that position during the ages, and must have reflected on the profound difference that exists between being at the foot of the rock of the Acropolis and being on the top of it. I, like the heroes of the past, began to feel my way round to find a gap in the defences.

At once I found myself in a maze of tiny houses that made Hampton Court's maze look like a wide-open space. And the paths between the houses were never more than four feet across, never ran for more than ten feet without at least one right-angle turn, usually had a large tree growing in the middle of it, and often was completely obstructed by a neighbourly party of local citizens, sitting round a table in the evening sun, drinking a glass of black wine, knitting, sewing, smoking, and exchanging the red-hot news of the day.

I don't think I've ever been more embarrassed in the whole of my life by the time I'd pushed my way through a dozen of these gossip-bees. I had to go forward after I'd pushed my way through a couple. To return and do my juggernaut-act a second time over the bodies of those courteous, smiling, but slightly bewildered groups, was unthinkable. And, mind you, I was dressed in a black, pin-striped, Savile Row suit, with an Anthony Eden hat, and, mind you, also, every hovel possessed a brown dog of mixed parentage and superlative inquisitiveness.

It was a journey which I enjoyed less than most other journeys that I can remember undertaking in my time.

But I struggled on. After all the damned Acropolis must have an opening somewhere, I felt. But kinking my neck to an unbelievable angle-like the pictures of these modern anti-aircraft guns that we see so far too often in the public prints nowadays — I could see part of a building which I knew must be the Erechtheum, and then, still kinking, I tripped over the roots of an olive-tree and fell heavily in front of a table at which six Hellenic damosels were having a quiet snort — as Dr. P. G. Wodehouse would put it.

It was not a moment at which even Walter Raleigh or Fersen or D'Orsay or Beau Nash would have shone with ease and elegance. The ladies fluttered and made little piping noises and dusted my clothes most charmingly, while I started to thank them in French, realized that French was no use, lost my head and rushed into broken Polish, realized that I had an olive twig in my hair and that I was holding the nearest object which I had grabbed in my fall — a very small brown Athenian puppy — remembered in a flash of intuition that Polish was an improbable medium of communication between myself and six fair Greekesses, and bolted round the next right-angle turn between the cottages.

Behind me arose a respectful murmur of feminine admiration at one so handsome, so strangely dressed, so obviously of the land-owning class, and so unjustly misfortunate, and in front of me was a broad concrete road up which the Athenian couples were wandering in the violet evening, to hold each other's hands or to circulate each other's waists or to see the view from the nearest point to the Parthenon to which an Athenian can attain nowadays without paying an entrance-fee of fifty drachmae. I had, in fact, circumnavigated the wall of the Acropolis at last.

My suit was covered with dust; my beautiful hat was battered in; my knees were sore; and, from a miserable yelping in my immediate vicinity, it was gradually borne in upon me that I was still holding the wretched pup in my elegant arms.

But all was worth it.

I was on the Acropolis at last, in an Athenian sunset.

I dropped the puppy, in a manner which might have drawn upon me some rather rude observations from an Inspector of the R.S.P.C.A., if one had chanced to be present, paid my fifty drachmae, and went up through the Propylaea to the Parthenon itself.

Well, what is there to say about the Parthenon that hasn't been said ten thousand times before? Describing things once again that everyone has read about *ad nauseam* is simply a bore. So don't be afraid. I'm not going to launch into a dithyramb about the honey-golden colour of the stone, or the proportions of the temple, or the tiny but all-important curves where the modern fatheaded architect makes a straight line, or the silent majesty of it (because often it is far from silent, especially when a Summer Cruise is in the Peiraeus), or any rot of that kind. It's all been done.

But what I am going to do is to say a word about the Parthenon as it has touched, from time to time, in two thousand five hundred years, a man or two, here and there.

Pericles was the man who commissioned the work and Ictinus was the architect who made it and Pheidias was the sculptor who adorned it.

Anonymous are the millions who adored its beauty, and it stood almost intact from 438 B.C. to A.D. 1687. Then another man with a name comes into its story, one Morosini, a Christian, a Venetian, a lover of beauty, a compatriot of Tintoretto and Giorgione, a citizen of the most exquisite and most lovingly praised of all the States that have been since Pericles commissioned his Parthenon.

Morosini sailed up the ancient sea-route past Aegina and Salamis and he landed his men, his Christian men, to fight against the infidel Turk.

The Turk had stored ammunition in the Parthenon, and it occurred to Signor Morosini, that beauty-loving Venetian, that a great coup was in his grasp. If he could only bombard the Turkish magazine with sufficient accuracy, he would explode it with a resounding detonation and thus strike a brave blow for the Cross against the Crescent.

The Venetian artillery was equal to the demands made upon it by its Commander, and a shell pitched into the magazine, and a great part of the supreme building of the world pitched outwards on its face in a jiffy.

But Morosini was a lover of beauty, as all Venetians are, and as soon as he had driven the Turks out of Athens, he set to work to repair some of the damage his shell had done. And there was only one way in which a Venetian could help to restore the glory of the Parthenon and that was the very obvious way of carting away the sculptures to Venice where they would be appreciated at their true worth by the Christian lovers of art.

So, having settled Ictinus, the architect, with a bomb, Morosini with his engineers turned his attention to Pheidias, the sculptor. These Venetian gentlemen tugged and hauled the great sculptures of the east pediment out of their place to lower them to the ground for transhipment to the Square of St. Mark's. Unfortunately their engineering skill seems to have been on a lower level than their undoubted love of art, and they dropped the sculptures to the ground where they were shattered to ten thousand fragments.

At that point Morosini fortunately gave up. He might have exercised his artistry and his lack of engineering skill upon the west pediment as well, in which case the next Figure in the tale would have found next to nothing to do. But Signor Morosini — like Mr. Robey — desisted. Perhaps he felt that, after all, Italian culture, as represented in this case by Venice, had done enough for glory. Perhaps he felt that they were only old pagan emblems anyway and that God, who had created Christianity to elevate the souls of men, had also created the Force of Gravity to make paganistic emblems descend.

But what does it matter? Morosini did in a twinkling what Time had not achieved in two thousand years. Perhaps Time did not want to achieve it. Perhaps Time wanted to mellow the Pentelican marble which Nature had produced.

Perhaps Time wanted to help Pheidias in his supreme creation. But what does it matter?

However, the Venetians were men of honour as well as men of a fine sensitivity in the matter of the arts. They had unluckily done somewhat of mischief to the Parthenon in the way of removing some of its beauty. So they set to work to compensate by adding something to it. They built, into the actual wall of the Parthenon, and soaring above it, a high, square tower. It is true that they didn't choose their material with quite the care that Ictinus and Pheidias chose theirs, and that they made their tower indiscriminately of rubble, bits of sculpture, stones from the Propylaea, old boots, or anything that came handy.

The point is that they, alone of all people, saw the fatal flaw in the building of Pericles.

"What's wrong with the Parthenon?" a hundred generations, puzzled, asked themselves.

"It's very nearly perfect, but not quite. What is it?" they said.

And then came Morosini who saw the answer in a flash. "It needs, to make it perfect, on the right-hand side of the entrance door, a handsome square tower built of old junk."

So he built it.

So much for Morosini. May he rot beside Lucius Mummius in hell!

And an old Jew millionaire from Hamburg passed by two hundred years later and had the vandalism to pull down the beautiful Venetian Tower. But then Herr Schliemann had the oddest ideas.

The next man who came along after Signor Morosini was our own Lord Elgin, and he also had Venetian ideas, and he also worked on Venetian principles. The first of these principles was that these wonderful treasures were not in safe-keeping; the Greeks, after all, were only trustees for them, responsible to the whole of the civilized world.

Principle Number Two was that there is only one safe spot in the whole of the civilized world for such treasures, and that spot is "somewhere else" — in Morosini's case Venice, in Elgin's London.

Elgin therefore, armed with this impenetrable shield of rectitude, cleverly got permission from the Sultan of Turkey to pull down the comparatively modern houses which were cluttering up the Acropolis, and to take away any sculptures and inscribed stones which he might find in them.

The Sultan, having signed the firman, thereupon turned over in his sleep, or massacred somebody, or married somebody, and Elgin got to work. It was child's play to alter the terms of his gift from the Sultan, and permission to take sculptures from modern houses was quickly extended to include permission to take sculptures from any house, and that, of course, included the Parthenon.

Nobody noticed, except the Greeks. And who cared about the Greeks anyway? And what had it got to do with them? The Sultan owned the Parthenon. London was the only fit place for Pheidias. Lord Elgin was the perfect intermediary.

So his lordship followed in Morosini's footsteps. Almost exactly.

He hired a squad of Italian workmen, gave them *carte blanche* to do what they liked, and himself departed. The Italian contractors were in fine form. They hit Pheidias for six in no time. The sculptures came rollicking down. When the cornice got in the way of the removal of half the south-western metopes, were his lordship's jolly, hokey-pokey contractors daunted? Not they. They simply threw down the cornice.

They had a brain-wave that something valuable might be hidden underneath the sweet, smooth pavement of the temple where Pericles and Socrates and Demosthenes and Plato and Aristotle must have walked. So they hoicked up one of the great white Pentelic blocks of marble to see. There was nothing there but the sandstone foundation, so it was labour wasted. But they didn't put the stone back. Why should they? The absentee lord was paying them on a time-contract. "Get me as much as you can in such-and-such a time for so much." That was Lord Elgin's bargain, and the chaps had to hurry.

So the sculptures, pediment, frieze, and metopes, have been saved for London. It is true that the Greeks kept them intact for two thousand years. It is true that they were given by a Turk to whom they did not belong to an Englishman to whom they did not belong.

But let us never forget that they have been saved from the Vandal Greek, and, still more important, from the dreadful Greek weather. They were never made — these Pentelic marbles — to withstand the sun of Greece. They were born for the gentle, homely, mild, soot-laden air of a Bloomsbury cellar. It is in smoke that Pheidias will live, not in sunshine. It is on the ground that his work is best appreciated, not skyed up on the pediment of a temple. In fact the man simply didn't know his job. But Lord Elgin knew it for him, and so to-day the sculpture is rightly called the Elgin Marbles, and not the Pheidias Sculpture, or the Parthenon Statues.

God! How I loathe the unctuous hypocrisy of the English.

I am too angry to write any more.

I will try again tonight after a bowl of Samian wine which I will certainly "dash down" as Byron remarked.

Yours in anger, R.

P.S. — Do you know what metopes are? They are the sculptures which run round the outside of the temple, near the top. Metope means a bandage round the forehead, which only shows that the Greeks were in advance even of Mademoiselle Lenglen.

Midnight on the same evening
Athens

I am restored to the sunniest of good-humour since I got back to my lovely cosmopolitan hotel and dashed down a couple of bowls, and watched from my discreet corner Mr. Michael Arlen and his beautiful wife holding court in the middle of the lounge, encompassed with attachés and their attachées, soldiers, men-of-the-world, and all the sort of characters who follow Mr. Oppenheim so sedulously from resort to resort.

The fact of the matter is that *The Times* has just arrived from London and it contains, amid its usual features of high sport and low politics, a whole lot of stuff about those very sculptures we were arguing about so hotly a few hours ago. As you, my poor little sap, never read anything but the pictures in the *Daily Mirror* and rely entirely for your views on every subject in the world upon the telephoned opinion of the silly mug who happens at the moment to be batting first for the Love-Sick Team, I will tell you the gist of Granny *Times'* red-hot news.

It appears that a few months ago the Trustees of the British Museum came to the conclusion that Lord Elgin's masterpieces wanted a wash-and-brush-up. The weather of London had got at them. (Precisely the same argument, as even you will notice, that his lordship used when he saw them in Athens. The only difference is the sort of weather. In his lordship's case two thousand years of sun had been at work. In the case of the Trustees, a hundred years of fog.)

So they set to, and again they followed his lordship's tradition. They dished the job out to some chaps, under a seventy-three-year-old foreman, and left them to it. The chaps, and the ancient, went to it in capital style.

Then after a month or two, a couple of other chaps, high up in the Museum service and working in the sculpture department, abruptly resigned. Well, that was that. Nothing much there, you will say. But half a moment. It was then officially stated that their resignation had nothing whatever to do with the cleaning of the Elgin Marbles.

Hullo, hullo, hullo, cried the boys, rubbing their eyes. What's all this? What's all this? Whoever said that their resignation had anything to do with the cleaning? Why this sudden and ingenuous disclaimer? The fox is bolted, but what fox is it?

Let us once again call the Poet Laureate to our help and cry:

> Oh, wind him! beauties, push him out,
> Yooi, on to him, Yahout, Yahout,
> Oh, push him out, Yooi, wind him, wind him."
> The beauties burst the scrub to find him.

It appears from the columns of Granny *Times* that rumours began to circulate, and that pointed questions began to be asked. But Brer Trustees lay low and said nothing. Their silence was tremendous. It was like the silence of the giraffe which has never been known to make a sound, even when small, bullied, sweated boys in the nineteenth century, before Shaftesbury, were sent down to sweep its throat (clearing its throat, as one might say). Or was it chimneys? I've forgotten. It was like the silence of a Quakers' Meeting which Charlie Lamb says is quieter than the uncommunicative muteness of fishes.

I don't for a moment mean that the Trustees are like fish. All I mean is that for two months they were dashed uncommunicating. They were remarkably mute. Then they unlimbered their battery and said that certain of the Marbles had been cleaned "in an unauthorized manner."

"In what manner?" screamed the entire Hunt, amid the yelping of the excited fox-dogs who by now "came romping at topmost speed" (Doc. Masefield again), but the Trustees had gone back under their shady rock in the fern-ringed pool and were not communicating anything more.

But the *Daily Express* — an independent hound — nosed about and finally flushed the aged foreman. "I cleaned the bad spots," cried the veteran, "with a copper tool which was softer than the marble."

So he too, that senior artificer, joins Morosini's men and Elgin's contractors in their niche of Pentelic marble.

Be a pet and drop into the Museum one day and see how the matter stands and send me a line. No, you can't do that because nothing in this world or the next, not even the certainty of the joint damnation of Morosini and Elgin, will make me give you my address. But go and see and put a description of them in Granny's Agony Column. It will reach me in about two years in the South Sea Islands.

And all this brings me gently and inevitably to the last of the men associated with the Acropolis in whom I am interested, that is to say, the tall and handsome gentleman, with an indefinable air of distinction, who was prowling round the place this evening. His suit was dusty, his hat was battered, but no one could mistake him for anything but the clean-limbed, well-tubbed Englishman that he was. My Father once remarked pensively of Sir William Ramsay, the famous archaeologist, as that learned gent was betaking himself down our ancestral avenue after a three hours' monologue on Acts xvi. 27-31:

> His boots are dust,
> His bike is rust,
> His soul is with St. Paul, I trust.

And so it was with me. Except that my soul was not in the least with that indefatigable letter writer whose two main achievements were firstly, that he invented a new religion which he called, for some reason, Christianity, and secondly that to this day he makes women wear hats in church.

My soul, if it was anywhere, was in the dim distant past when, as an urchin of repellent aspect, like all urchins, and of nauseating manners, I used to play "Hector and Achilles" or follow breathlessly, Theseus on his excursion to Athens.

There's no use my saying that Memory is a queer thing. It's been said before. But as I stood on the north side of the Parthenon and looked over Attica, things came back to me which I swear hadn't been in my mind for thirty years. I could tell the names — bit by bit — of everything I could see. Lycabettus, of course, was easy, and so was Hymettus where the honey comes from. But how did I remember the gap between Pentelicus and Hymettus where the road runs from Athens to Marathon?

How did I remember Parnes? Or that the lowest road, the one on the left, is the pass of Daphne and goes to Eleusis, opposite Salamis?

And even the story of Daphne came back to me, and a most instructive story it is too. She was a pretty girl who went out of her way to pester Phoebus Apollo. He, being a normal, decent chap, made the advances towards her which she was angling for. And then, of course, she went all fluttering and coy and pretended to try to escape. Apollo, bored to death — naturally — played up and pursued her. But, just as she was deliberately letting him catch her, she made a fatal mistake. She prayed for assistance — not meaning it for a moment — to Zeus, and Zeus — honest old donkey — took her at her word and changed her into a laurel-tree, which the Greeks call Daphne to this day. And here is the point of the story, which no one in all classical study has ever noticed except me — and I only noticed it this evening — from that instant the laurel-tree became Apollo's favourite shrub.

And why? Was it because it reminded him of a girl who had repulsed his advances and screamed for help at the critical moment just as if he had been the traditional Fiend with Hatchet Slays Six? Would *that* make a man romantically all sentimental about a rather boring evergreen which is seldom seen nowadays outside North and West London's suburbs? Of course not. The solution is an elementary one and a human one, the two adjectives being interchangeable and synonymous. Apollo made the laurel his favourite tree because of his narrow escape. When the frolicsome, twittering Daphne was suddenly transformed into a daphne, Apollo stood back, mopped his brow, and murmured, "Thank Zeus for that," and regarded the laurel with deep and grateful affection for ever after.

And you, my small piece of nonsense, are my laurel-tree. I regard you, as I too mop my brow, as an admirable shrub. And Thank Zeus for it.

Over on the right was Laurium, where the silver came from, and behind me Salamis again. It was an evening of one's dreams. "The pale pure Attic air," as Mahaffy, that learned and comic Irishman, once observed. And for the first time I realized the meaning of "violet-crowned." As usual the Greeks had a word for it, and as usual the word was the perfect one. The Athenian evening is violet. Everything, mountains, sky, sea, valleys, buildings, olive-woods, flowers, all are crowned with violet.

> All the world is sweeter, if the Athenian violet quicken:
> All the world is brighter, if the Athenian sun return.

(For your benefit, Swinburne.)

If only the Athenians had not used the same adjective for Aphrodite as well. They called that girl violet-crowned as well as their beloved city. It was a sad mistake. But what can you expect of a people who were so obsessed with you that they called their beloved city after a woman, and dedicated their great temple to grey-eyed Athena and called it the Parthenon, the Maiden's Temple?

Her favourite bird was the Owl. No wonder.

The moment this idea struck me, as I was standing on the wall and looking across at the Areopagus where the Epistolary Paul was puzzled by that simplest and most obvious of inscriptions, "To the Unknown God," I was filled with a great annoyance. Must it follow me everywhere, this Unknown Goddess? Is Athene Parthenos to dog me for ever, hand in hand with Aphrodite and that fool Hera, who must have been a Circassian for cow-like stupidity? (Homer calls her ox-eyed, and I bet he knew.)

When I reach Decelea it is Venus who rises arrogantly over the mountain. On the Acropolis every stick and stone is dedicated to a woman. Even the lovely miniature temple which they call the Erechtheum is supported by Caryatids (except for one vacancy where little Mr. Elgin did his stuff) and it was used by a Turkish viceroy as his harem — God help him. Everywhere women, women, women.

With a sort of vague fear in my heart at this all-pervading web, I turned once again in the direction of Mount Parnes and looked down at the wheat-golden temple which they call the Theseum — the temple of Theseus — and my spirits rocketed up again.

There was a man for you. No nonsense about him. He knocked out Sciron in a round or two; he dealt smartly with Procrustes, and Sinis, and the Crommyonian sow (no false chivalry there, my girl), and knew exactly what to do with the Cretan bull when he met him in the Labyrinth. Joselito, the young and adored Espada who died in the Plaza de Toros at Talavera del Reina in 1920, was nothing to Theseus. Joselito needed capadores, and picadores, and banderilleristas, and all the paraphernalia of the bull-fight, before he could polish off the exhausted animal. And even with all that, a bull got him in the end.

But Theseus did it single-handed. He went into the Labyrinth with his sword and came out intact. And what's more, he was adored just as much as Joselito ever was, but he kept his head. Ariadne fell for him in Crete and she was the daughter of a King, which, so far as I've ever heard, is somewhat higher than Joselito ever got. But Theseus was not dazzled. He accepted her help in the matter of the reel of thread, but flatly refused to accept the typically feminine theory that the gift of a reel of thread ought to be repaid with a lifetime of slavery. So he left her, and in my opinion rightly, in Naxos, where Dionysus found her and amused himself for a couple of hours.

The only thing which I regret about the whole manly, virile story, is that it provided Tintoretto with the chance to produce one of his less fortunate canvases.

So the Theseum is the antidote to the Parthenon. Athens was not always entirely obsessed by you. I could hold up my head again and think some amused little thoughts about that other Naxos, just behind the BBC in London. How's, Dionysus these days? Pretty good?

I drifted back in the twilight with my mind filled with violet crowns and olive-trees, "greyleaved and glimmering," and the strange worship of women which has afflicted so many pretty men.

I have a last bowl of Samian in my hand. Here's your health, Theseus. You and I know what's what. Only I hope a new Tintoretto won't paint a masterpiece of my Ariadne, "Ariadne in Mayfair." It would be too good for her, even if it was a real Tintoretto.

And so, daughter of Minos and dealer in reels of thread, I salute you gaily, coolly, and genteelly, and take my leave of you. R.

P.S. — It is recorded that Medea, the dark witch-lady, tried to poison Theseus and failed. Do you believe in, reincarnation? Good-bye, Daph.

P.P.S. — Byron says somewhere in *Don Juan* that Humboldt, the traveller, had a machine called a cyanometer; Byron goes on to describe it:

> An airy instrument, with which he sought
> To ascertain the atmospheric state,
> By measuring "the intensity of blue";
> Oh! Lady Daphne! let me measure you.

9th April, 1939
Somewhere Over Europe

I dodged away from you this morning in a panic. I awoke at the crack of dawn in a cold perspiration, realizing that you knew Michael Arlen and that it would be child's play for you to get in touch with him by wireless and find out all my plans. I could see you sitting at Croydon, pensively watching an aeroplane being warmed up for you, while your deadly, clear eyes surveyed a map of the world and your coral-pink ear nestled against a long-distance telephone receiver, thereby hallowing for all time that bit of old vulcanite.

I bounced out of bed and yelled for help. The Steward, who was presumably dreaming of the Siege of Leyden at the end of the corridor, bounced out of his bed and woke the Captain, who certainly was not dreaming of the Siege of Haarlem, and the Captain woke the Engineer who was dreaming of piston-rods, and Sparks who was dreaming of the Morse Code for "Darling" in Dutch, and the Second Officer who was dreaming of the best way to cross a Rembrandt tulip with an ordinary Darwin, and in two hours we had scampered out to Decelea, satisfied the officials that we had less money than ever and no artillery, and that we still hadn't caught smallpox, and darted off for "an unknown destination."

Venus was still in the sky but she was a poor ghost of a planet, very pale and unself-confident. It was an encouraging omen. She was so blatantly aggressive last night, over Decelea, haunt of jackboots. Now she is just a wisp. Treat you rough, that's the style.

With a nasty sneer from all of us, and a curl of the lip in the direction of the old girl — except for Sparks, who kissed his silly hand to her, — we thundered across the Air-Harbour and rose into the Aegean wind.

Hymettus was dark and dusty, but I swear a shaft of dawn sunlight flickered for a moment over the Theseum. The old boy was winking to me and wishing me luck.

Another stage in the Flight from a Lady had begun, and in a moment we were rounding Cape Sunium, and steering north. Safe once again, high in the pale Attic air.

In a jiffy we were looking down on the mountains which look on Marathon, which, in turn, if you remember, looks on the sea. Byron dreamed that Greece might yet be free. I don't have to dream. I know that I am free. No one, neither you nor anyone else, is going to deem me a slave.

I can't see Tanagra and I'm not sorry. There was a time, about fifty years ago, when I used to think that you looked, occasionally, like a Tanagra figure. You had a trick — laboriously learnt, I have no doubt, at the School of Dramatic Art or at Italia Conti's — of falling into an attitude of such sweet, simple grace that nothing except one of those Tanagra statuettes could be put beside you. And even those little masterpieces seemed almost clumsy in comparison. You had a beauty. I'm a fair-minded man, and I'm not going to deny that you had a beauty. You don't mean anything, any more, but you were beautiful.

So I'm not flying over Tanagra. There are plenty of other things in the world to think about than terra-cotta figurines and the sweet grace of your attitudes.

We're over Thermopylae, but there is nothing to see. It's the place where the wooden-heads put on their armour and fought to the death against the Persians. History writes it down as a spectacular example of heroism, and Simonides wrote a moving epitaph about the three hundred men who died there.

Actually it was a battle between three hundred disciplined Prussians (they called them Spartans in those days; different name, same men) and a few million undisciplined Persians, who were just vague but dangerous barbarians. It was organized savagery against disorganized.

The Prussians were swamped in the end because they hadn't the elementary common sense to discover that their position was outflanked by a road across the hills. But they combed their hair before the battle, and fought, and earned four lines from Simonides, and go down into history. Silly asses. Prussians are always silly asses.

Now the Captain is pulling out over the Bay of Pagasai and another of my dreams is coming true. Down there is the little town where, for me, all history began. Down there is the first, translucent spring of romance. Down there — we are cruising very slowly now — is the tiny cluster of white houses whence came one of the three great stories of the, world. One story was made about the tenth year of the Siege of Troy. The second was about the return from Troy of the King of Ithaca. And from that tiny patch of dwellings in the Bay of Pagasai, which I can see so clearly in the dawn, came the third. For it was from Iolcos-by-the-Sea that Jason set out in the Argo to find the Golden Fleece.

It was there, three thousand feet below me, at Iolcos-by-the-Sea, that the Heroes came together, from all parts of Hellas, and built their ship and fixed the Dodonian oak-branch to the prow and made their sacrifice to Hera — the poor fools — and set out to "win undying fame." It is all written down in Kingsley's book, except the moral of it.

You won't find the moral in Kingsley's book, because Kingsley wasn't concerned with such things. But I know the moral, and I'm telling it to you now. It's this. The Heroes put their faith in Hera and got what they deserved. Hera, the Queen of Olympus, the ox-eyed. And she was a fine patroness of a boating excursion if ever there was one.

The Heroes really worshipped her. They went down on their knees at the mention of her name. They prayed to her. They sacrificed to her. They thought she was the Top. And just look how she rewarded them. Let me remind you of one or two incidents in their story.

The first thing which happened to the Heroes on their voyage in the Argo was that they were attacked one night in their sleep by some very large men who had six arms and "lived with the bears in the mountains." No sooner had they successfully dealt with this remarkable foray — at the trifling expense of their host whom Hercules killed by mistake in the confusion and the darkness — than they got caught up in a whirlwind. That was a bad start. Then Hercules went ashore with his boyfriend, and the boyfriend got pinched by some water-nymphs and taken down to the bottom of their lake "to be their playfellow for ever," which, considering all the circumstances, must have turned out to be a bit of a sell for the water-nymphs. I mean, you can't be a boyfriend to a lout like Hercules and amuse water-nymphs as well. There's a limit to versatility in these our days, and presumably there was a limit to versatility in those their days.

To continue the tale. Hercules got worked up into such a state of agitation over his little chum that he went and lost himself in the woods and had to be left behind by the Heroes, who were in a hurry to make a dig at the Golden Fleece — and I don't blame them, and I know that you wouldn't blame them either who've made a dig at any gold that was about and around, whether the fleece came from Colchis or Australia. Haven't you?

So Hercules was left behind. And what was Hera doing, that lady-protector of brave men? Nothing.

The next to go were Zetes and Calais, the sons of the North Wind, who openly deserted the troops and went off to fight the Harpies.

Did the all-powerful Hera stop them? Not she. The Harpies were girls too — all Harpies are — and Hera, being a girl herself, was only too delighted at the thought that the Sons of the North Wind were off to spend a lifetime in harrying other members of her sex.

So Zetes and Calais vanish from the tale.

Next came the turn of Idmon who died "of an evil sickness" and a wild boar killed Tiphys, the steersman.

But all this was child's play compared with what happened when the boys reached Colchis and made the acquaintance of a girl called Medea. She was a sweet little piece and no mistake. As soon as Jason had collared the Golden Fleece, and made a bolt for his home-town, he found that Medea was coming along too. ("Where the gold is, there the girl lies also," as Browning almost remarked.) Medea's father, quite reasonably, went after the thieves. He didn't want his daughter, but he did want the Fleece. He was a man with a sound sense of proportion. He knew what was valuable and what wasn't. But Medea had a standard of values too, and when the pursuers came too near, she chopped up her little brother, whom she'd taken along with her, just in case of emergencies — for she was a woman of long views — and threw the bits overboard and so stopped the pursuit — her father, who was leading it, being a sentimental man by all accounts and much moved by the sight of the floating remains of his son.

After that the Heroes had an assortment of varied misfortunes which landed them as far south as the Red Sea and as far north as the Baltic.

The next Hero to go astray was Butes, but he asked for it. He swam ashore on the Island of Anthemousa, the flowery island, and knelt in front of the Siren-ladies and was just on the point of getting what he deserved when he fell out of the frying-pan into the fire and was snatched away by Aphrodite and deposited for some reason on the peak of Lilybaeum "where he slept many a pleasant year." A bizarre finish.

Lots more trouble followed. Canthus went ashore in Libya to steal some sheep and was killed by a stone thrown at him by the shepherd, just as another shepherd, a ruddy youth, killed Goliath with a stone.

Mopsus, the ornithologist of the party, trod on a snake and he was the last casualty before the Heroes — middle-aged men now, tired, salt-caked, bowlegged with too much rowing, bronzed, bearded, and bewildered — came back at last to Iolcos-by-the-Sea.

Fun and games were still in store for these protégés of Hera. Medea killed pretty nearly everyone before she was through, including her own children, and Hercules turned up again mysteriously with some more of his poisoned arrows which did a lot of damage as usual, and at last only Nestor was left and the worst fate of all was reserved for him. For he survived to be the most crashing bore in the whole history of literature, including Polonius and Meredith's Egoist.

Well did Jason cry to Medea (at least I suppose he did; it's in Dr. Gilbert Murray's translation) "O Stone of women."

But I think the Heroes might have said the same about Hera.

In fact we can all of us say it about all of you.

.   .   .   .   .

And now I am swinging lazily out to sea again, along what Kingsley called "the long Magnesian shore." I think that is the earliest phrase which I can remember hearing spoken, and it has haunted me all my life. The snow mountains on my left are Pelion and Ossa, and in the distance I can see Olympus.

You were on Olympus once, you silly little girl. You sat in the Hall of the Immortals, and made eyes at Ares, and infuriated Aphrodite and answered Athena with smart repartee, and had prayers said to you every hour of the day. You too were the Queen of the World.

But now no longer. Oh dear me no.

Olympus used to be a block of flats behind the BBC.

Now it's gone back to the long Magnesian shore where it was in the old days of imaginary goddesses.

And imaginary goddesses are the only real ones. The others are a bore. They always turn out simply to deserve a block of flats behind the BBC. And I can't say worse than that. You are always likely to run into an Announcer in a bad temper. But Olympus is superb. It is high and it is cold and it is serene and it is far away, and it never has existed except in the hearts of poets. None of you have ever existed except in the hearts of poets.

The greatest of living poets has written:

> What are the names for Beauty? Who shall praise
> God's pledge he can fulfil His creatures' eyes?
> Or what strong words of what creative phrase
> Determine Beauty's title in the skies?
> But I will call you Beauty Personate,
> Ambassadorial Beauty, and again
> Beauty triumphant, Beauty in the Gate,
> Beauty salvation of the souls of men.

> For Beauty was not Beauty till you came
> And now shall Beauty mean the sign you are;
> A Beacon burnt above the Dawn, a flame
> Like holy Lucifer the Morning Star,
> Who latest hangs in Heaven and is the gem
> On all the widowed Night's expectant Diadem.

That is what I used to feel about you, in the days when you were crowned with glory on Olympus.

I've told the Captain to cram on all the speed he's got in his Douglas engines. I'm tired of the sight of Olympus. It reminds me of things I don't want to remember. I once had a Faith, and I've lost it, and that's that.

And things lost never come back. One of the loveliest and the most mournful of lines in the English language is a question to which there is only one answer,

Will they ever come back to me, ever again, the long, long dances?

And the answer is "No."

And no man outside a loony-bin wants them back again. You can catch the fragrance of syringa only once in your life, the first time, and you can only lie once with all your senses "in meadows drowsy with Trinacrian bees." Only the fools want again to dance the long, long dances. Strike out the old tunes. Grab a new dancing-partner from some one. Throw her away when the dance is over, and grab another one. Nothing matters, nothing, except keeping abreast of the times, looking at the future, forgetting the dances of the past and the Olympus where we used to worship, and coming down into a Palais de Danse in some jolly, vulgar suburb.

Good-bye, Olympus. You once had a real goddess. The Douglas engines are turning over a nice two hundred and twenty miles an hour and Salonica will be in sight in a moment.

. . . . .

I hate Salonica.

So far as I'm concerned, two men have ruined Salonica for me. The first, of course, was the egregious Paul, who wrote two of his letters to the unhappy citizens. And the second was Sarrail, the French General who was given the command of the Allied armies there in the War.

The Germans called Salonica their largest internment camp, because half a million men of the Allies did nothing there for years. Sarrail was in command. He was under the impression that he had saved Verdun; he had a great talent for political intrigue; and his mistress at Salonica — for she accompanied him upon his military adventures — often exclaimed, in despair, that if only she was allowed to issue a few orders things would soon begin to move.

I think you would have made a good commander at Salonica. Whatever your defects — and Heaven knows you have plenty — when you begin to issue orders, things do begin to move.

. . . . .

We're flying over the Vardar gorge, and now we're coming out over the green fields of the plain of Serbia. There are little squares of trees which I think must be orchards, and lots of sheep in pens, but only a few isolated houses. The people seem to live in villages hereabouts. It isn't worth while swerving over to the right to see the Iron Gates of the Danube, because they are a grossly over-rated spectacle.

Nor is it worthwhile swerving over to look at the Kazan Defile, though the Defile is incomparably more majestic than the Gates, when you see it from a Danube steamer. But from the air you get a very poor perspective of small heights. The Himalayas are all right, I expect, but anything much lower simply looks flat.

The Kazan Defile from the steamer is a superb gorge of the river. But from the air it would be nothing. Besides, I wouldn't be able to see the really exciting things about it — the cuttings in the rock where Trajan's legions built their wooden road, along the foot of the precipice and jutting over the water, and the inscription, traced out on the wall of the precipice, to commemorate the passing that way of Trajan and his men, on his Dacian campaign in — when? — I don't know, but then nor do you, so let's make a shot at it and say eighteen hundred years ago.

I've got a theory about landscape, that pretty nearly all of it is a bore unless it's associated with human beings. I think of Everest as the place where Mallory died, and of the North Pole as the place that Nansen nearly went to in the "Fram," and of the upper Amazon as the river where the local lepidopterae tried so forlornly to bite Peter Fleming to death. I can't rave about a field of buttercups except by imagining that they might look like the shield of Achilles.

About a hundred years ago, shortly after Victoria stamped her foot and uttered her most memorably incorrect prediction, "I *will* be good," I went down with you to a country club somewhere in Hertfordshire. My only recollection of the place is that you were there. The rest has vanished.

So it is with the Kazan. Unless I can read Trajan's inscription, I don't want to see the pseudo-romantic precipices with their swirling waters. But where Trajan went, and where you used to go, there was nothing pseudo. Those were the high moments of the world.

Belgrade is white in the morning sun in front of me, and there are moments when even the Danube — that ridiculous invention of one of the Strauss brothers (no human being except perhaps their Mother and themselves has ever been able to distinguish between the three of them) — takes on a faintly blue appearance.

I think I'll stop for a quick lunch at Belgrade, although I don't like the people and I don't like the place. But I am hungry, and the plum-brandy which they call Slivovitz — or words to that effect — has unquestionable merits. I used to drink it, years ago, in the bar of the Sacher Hotel in Vienna, under the cold, tough eyes of Frau Sacher, with her black cigar and her fleet of French bulldogs and her halo of legendary sanctity which only gilds the heads of women who have been in their heyday the mistresses of Emperors.

I suppose it's more practical, from the worldly point of view, to be the mistress of an Emperor than the wife of an artist, and women are nothing if not practical. When the romance is over, the Frau Sachers can retire, if they've been prudent, with a hotel and a few strings of diamonds and some tiaras, and live in comparative luxury for the rest of their lives.

On the other hand the wife of the artist probably has a wretched time with an irritating, egotistical, nervous creature who harasses her in her mortal life and makes her immortal hereafter.

And what is the good of that to any woman? A comfortable home is worth a lot more than a niche in Valhalla.

But the trouble is that no artist can ever understand that.

"Marry me," he cries, "and I will put you beside Helen and Beatrice."

"I'd sooner have a house in Carlton Gardens," replies the girl coldly, and the artist is baffled. He can't make it out.

And so with you and me. I was baffled for years. But I've got the hang of it at last. You will fetch up in the end with your tiaras and your French bulldogs, and in fifty years no one will remember your name.

Well, it's your choice, and I expect you're right. Belgrade is at my feet and I want to have lunch.

.   .   .   .   .   .

I've said it before, and I'll say it again. I don't like the Serbs.

They outraged the conscience of the world when they put up their monument to Gavrile Princep who fired the shot at Sarajevo which started the World War; they extinguished, cynically, Montenegro; they are steadily extinguishing the Croats. They are, in fact, a nasty mess.

But the Slivovitz was fiery and enheartening, and Belgrade is a city of fine memories.

The most loyal of all soldiers won his laurels at Belgrade, and Marlborough might have found his work more difficult if Eugene had not smashed the Turks and gained European renown by the capture of this glittering town on the banks of the Danube.

The victory of Eugene against the Infidel made it possible for Marlborough and the Dutch to join in the great defence against Louis XIV. And here I am, talking about the Dutch again. I expect that the Steward is dreaming about Oudenarde, and the Second Pilot is dreaming about Ramillies. We all know, of course, what Sparks is thinking about. And no mortal being can say what the Captain is thinking about.

I had thought of pushing on to Budapest, but now I'm not so sure. We are still flying northwards up the Danube, but I'm beginning to waver. I have so many happy memories of Central Europe in the old, gay days before castor-oil and the rubber truncheon became part of the standard life of so many countries. Central Europe won't be a place for gaiety for quite a while now.

Budapest was a lovely town once. I expect that it still looks lovely, but I wonder if the folk laugh quite as much as they used to, or in quite so carefree a style. Slovakia is very near them, and so is Vienna.

No, I'm not going on. I can't bear the thought of seeing Vienna or the dark shadows of the Bohemian Forest. I once walked all day in the Forest and drank beer at little open-air cafés and listened to the songs of the passers-by. Even if people still sing in the Bohemian Forest I couldn't sing with them. I couldn't hold up my head high enough to sing if any Czechs or Slovaks were about. They might ask me what a British Guarantee really did mean. They might look at me with mournful eyes and murmur that the British are great boys when it comes to Freedom and Democracy, and ask how Dr. Beneš is getting on in America, and is it true that Lord Runciman is enjoying the best of health, and if so, then they are all delighted to hear it.

In the old happy days Central Europe was the cynosure of those few British eyes which had a gleam of intelligence in them. It was the Dog's-Tail, which is what Cynosure means. But I'm galloping ahead. You wouldn't understand. So I'll explain.

The Cynosure was the Greek name for the Small Bear in the velvet Hellenic sky. It was so brightly radiant in the Heavens — as you were once so brightly radiant in my Heaven, so that you *were* my Heaven — that all the lads and maidens, in Greece, on their gentle philanderings, when they were "gravelled for lack of matter," looked up at the Dog's-Tail. Thus the Cynosoura of those lovely, long-ago, starlit nights has become now our cynosure.

In fact, what the Greeks called the Dog's-Tail, the American used to call in the slang of a few years ago the Cat's Whiskers. It's the same idea. As I was saying, in the sweet days Central Europe was our magic grotto. It was our silver-encrusted pavilion of romance. It was there that we knew we would find the field of Austerlitz, and Schönbrunn, and the Spanische Hofreitschule, and the pictures in the Lichtenstein Gallery, and Balaton, and gipsies and violins and Mozart, and Grinzing with its small and lovely vintage of last year's wine which they call Heurigen, and the rock of Salzburg, and the laughter which used to ripple unendingly among the lakes and the mountains of the Salzkammergut.

It was unfair of us — and we knew it. But we resolutely put the unfairness out of our minds. The mark tumbled, and the Austrian crown tumbled, and the Hungarian crown tumbled, and we brandished our pound notes and wallowed in the misfortunes of others.

We bought their wine for a few pence and their cigars for a farthing and their theatre tickets for an old song, and boasted about it, while they were half-starved and desperately frightened for the future. But they never once reproached us for our profiteering and our arrogance — and never, through all the semi-starvation and the fear, did the sound of laughter entirely die away in the Salzkammergut.

It is unbelievable to think of now. In those days we had just finished fighting a bloody war against those very people. We had been trained on Europe's pet curriculum of Hatred. We had been told by innumerable fat sergeant-majors and over-Kümmelled major-generals that there was no good Hun except a dead Hun, and that went for Austrians and Hungarians and Bulgars, but not, inscrutably, for the Turks ("A gentlemanly fighter is old Johnny Turk").

Yet, as soon as it was all over we flocked across to the lands of the savages and found them not so very savage after all.

A few pounds was enough for a couple of weeks in Vienna, and for a few shillings one could voyage in a languid steamer from Passau to Constanza, through the green plains that I am flying over at this moment.

But all, all has vanished, and the long, long dances will not come back in my time. Europe's Hatred has re-established itself, and two men who didn't fight in the World War because they were cowards have contrived to outwit the generosity and good-will of several million fighting men of whom so many made friends with each other in the woods and cafés and gardens of Central Europe.

Good-bye, Vienna, I shall never see you again. Sobieski saved you from the Turks, but even Gentleman Johnny might have been a better master than the swine of the Gestapo.

So I won't go any further. This is a Flight to Freedom. Slavery lies behind. About turn, Captain. We'll turn our backs upon Tyranny, whether it is German or Italian or feminine. All brands of Tyranny are hateful. Down with all Tyrants, whether they are sons of blacksmiths in black shirts, or sadistic house-painters in brown shirts, or just you (No, I'm not talking to you, Captain, now. Sorry).

About ship, Captain. Put the helm hard over. Steward, uncork the flask of Slivovitz that I bought from that rascally Serb and bring glasses. I'll give you a toast.

Ready? To every man who has fought for Freedom. What did you say, Steward? "And to hell with the Duke of Alva"?

Certainly. Fill up again. And to hell with the Duke of Alva, man or woman. That's the style.

Captain. Back to Greece. To-night I shall sleep underneath the stars in the honey-laden air upon the beach of Marathon, and wake to hear the laughter of the sounding sea.

This is no air for free men. You can see the stinking mephitic clouds of slavery down there. We'll keep our silver wings bright in the sun. R.

P.S. — I shall post this letter from the village post-office at Marathon. Get the post-mark framed and hang it above your bed to remind you that Tyrants do not always win.

10th April, 1939
Over the Greek Islands

I don't need to tell you that I spent the night after all in the nice, comfortable, cosmopolitan hotel in Athens. It suddenly occurred to me that the beach at Marathon might be haunted by mosquitoes as well as by the ghosts of brave free men, and that perhaps the scent of honey wasn't really more fragrant in the open dusty air than over an air-conditioned breakfast-table.

Besides, I never was much of a one for *al fresco* entertainment. Give me the many-cushioned divan and anyone who wants can have the heathery couch or the prickly roots of last year's ferns.

We started again at dawn and swept superbly out across the islands, heading south this time, south and east.

Soon we came to the Isles of Greece where burning Sappho twanged her lyre and so on. I don't propose to pull out as far east as Lesbos itself because I don't hold with that girl's mode of life. She was a wow of a poet, but I don't have to go to Lesbos to read her poetry.

"Evening star, thou bringest back all things which the bright dawn has scattered; thou bringest the lamb, thou bringest the goat, thou bringest the little child to its mother."

Yes, she was a poet all right, one of the half-dozen that your ethereal, delicate, sensitive sex has produced in two or three thousand years. Sensitive my foot! Ethereal my eye!

The reason why you can't write poetry or paint or sew or cook or design dresses or invent dances or, in fact, contribute to the dreams of the world, is because you are all hard, tough materialists, with your sweet little feet firmly planted on the ground (or, more likely, on a man's neck) and not the vestige of a cloud about your heads. Sappho was a freak, and so was Elizabeth Browning, and so was Angelica Kauffmann. And don't start putting up the plaintive old squeak that women can't create anything beautiful because they've never had a square deal in education, and that after a few generations of Somerville and Girton you'll be turning out a regular flood of Rembrandts and Shelleys. More likely a regular flood of Ouidas and Ella W. Wilcoxes.

No, the plain truth is that you're no good. We've passed Ceos where Simonides the poet was born, and a tiny little island which was the most sacred of all the shrines, Delos, home of the Delian Apollo, more sacred even than Delphi, and we're coming to Paros where they quarried the marble which was used for the roof of the Parthenon, because the light could filter through it more easily than through Pentelican, and Naxos where Theseus so wisely dumped Ariadne before she had completely ruined his life.

Over on the right is the barren rock of Seriphos on which Perseus and his mother were washed up in their boat. (She was a nice, typical girl too. She flatly refused to have anything to do with Zeus so long as he was just a plain, honest, decent chap who made honest, decent advances to her, in one of his repertory parts, as a bull or a swan. But the moment he, in despair, had the brilliant notion of turning himself into a shower of gold, Danaë surrendered — as it is quaintly called — in a trice. She would go far on the films today.)

Beyond Seriphos there is Melos, where the statue was found of the lady without arms. Classical experts for many years have wondered how the arms were posed in the statue. One thing is certain. They were not being used by their owner to hold up the exiguous garment which is slipping so innocently to the ground.

When a girl gets as far as that Melian girl in the way of undressing, she doesn't fuss about the final stages. My own solution of the problem is that she was holding a sawn-off shot-gun in her right hand, fully loaded, and extending the left, palm upwards, in the traditional style of Danaë and the rest.

But let us be fair. When a girl has gone that far, she is entitled to a shower of gold, isn't she? Or isn't she?

The Cyclades are falling behind us now. The Aegean is infinitely blue, and the sun has risen high, and the last but one of the rocky islands is Anaphae, dark and wooded, with a ringlet of white where the tideless sea makes its impotent protest against the rocks, and the last of all is Carpathos.

We could, of course, go across to Rhodes and refill with petrol near the fortress where the Christian Knights made their immortal defence against the Saracens. But that would once more involve me with Signor Mussolini and his be-garlicked heroes in dirty old plus-fours, so I will steer for the open sea.

I can see the snow of Mount Ida on Crete above Cnossos, the town of the Minotaur that Theseus dealt with so firmly, and as we cruise past Cape Ampelus, the south-westernmost point of Crete, I realize that I am gazing for the very last time upon a bit of Europe.

In a few moments Europe will have dropped away into the mists at two hundred miles an hour, and I for one will be heartily glad of it.

Since there's no help, Europe, come let us kiss and part —

> Nay I have done, you get no more of me;
> And I am glad, yea, glad with all my heart
> That thus so clearly I myself can free.

And don't run away, Europe, with the idea that just because the first four lines of Drayton's sonnet are applicable to our situation, yours and mine, that the last two lines are also applicable.

> Now if thou would'st, when all have given him over,
> From death to life thou might'st him yet recover.

None of that now, Europe, you old harridan. Don't try any of your funny games on me. You're just wasting your time.

Cretan snows and rocks have gone. Europe no more.

Ave atque Vale, you venerable slut, you Aphrodite of Bethnal Green.

. . . .

Now there is nothing beneath us but the bluest water I have ever seen, and I have time to think a little.

Ought I to feel remorse and the so-called pangs of ingratitude at shaking the dust, and mud, and lava of Europe off my feet for ever? Has she done so much for me that I owe her anything in return? What is she, after all?

She started life as a very beautiful girl — whence the origin of all woe, universally and to eternity — who found a gentle, tame bull on the seashore when she was disporting herself with her handmaidens, probably in the usual way that girls disport themselves on seashores when there are no men about — by throwing catches to each other with a soft india-rubber ball and missing every catch and screaming shrilly to each other with high unintelligible cries.

Europa, the fat-headed ninny, found the bull so charming, so like our modern Ferdinand, that she delicately clambered on to its back. Whereupon it very naturally — as any simpleton could have predicted — turned out to be old Papa Zeus in one of his innumerable fancy-dresses, and not in the least like Ferdinand, and the next thing the silly girl discovered was that he had swum with her on his back to Crete, and that, once they reached the island, if she was on anybody's back it certainly was no longer his. My little dictionary says that "Modern writers, though without very sure grounds, have interpreted Europa to be a moon-goddess."

By Heavens, those modern writers — grey-bearded dotards by now, according to the date of my dictionary — were nearer the mark than they thought. I — a much more modern writer than any of them — know positively that Europa was a moon-girl (not a goddess, of course. There never were real goddesses until that evening in the country years ago when we walked in the moonlight, and there have been none since I walked out on you last week at the Ritz) .

But Europa was a simple moon-girl, and Europe has ever after been her loony-bin.

Well, that was the start of the Continent. Not a very dignified start.

But much worse has followed. You don't need to bother to look into a history-book, my little illiterate, in order to dig up interminable stories of battle and devastation and cruelty and torture and murder. Just think for a moment of the Europe that I have known myself at first hand in my short life.

A Continent of war, and slums, and armaments, and underfeeding for the poor and overfeeding for the rich, a Continent of concentration-camps and oppression and injustice, a Continent of misery and hatred and fear, where no laughter can be. That's what Europe is to-day.

Britain and France may stand a little apart at the moment, and Scandinavia and Belgium and Switzerland, and the ever-green, ever-irrigated Holland. But very soon they may be engulfed in the maelstrom.

And in many ways even Britain and France must take their share of the hatreds and the cruelties. The industrial revolution left an England and a Scotland which are mighty poor fun for the poor, and mighty good fun for the rich. The dispro-portion of wealth is almost as great in Britain as it was in France in the eighteenth century and in Russia in the nineteenth, and where did that disproportion land the Monarchy and the Tsardom?

And with it goes the everlasting stupidity of the rich, the maddening stupidity of the rich. There is always a case to be made out for the rule of aristocracy, if the aristocrats are really "the Best People," as in the Greek word. But we haven't got aristocracy. What we've got is upper-middle-class plutocracy, and that is the real scum of the earth with its abysmal selfishness and its everlasting counting of its wretched money-bags for fear lest a hundredth part of one-per-cent has been filched from them, and its genuine belief that a waistcoat made out of a Union Jack is the hallmark of patriotism. How I hate and despise them.

When I was a very small boy these upper-middle-plutodemocrats brought off one of their most characteristic coups. They fought a righteous war of self-defence against a treacherous, powerful, aggressive nation. I remember it well. I was brought up on it.

I watched the City Imperial Volunteers marching to that war amid the frenzied cheers of the multitude to which I added my small and super-patriotic squeak; I stuck pins in a map which I didn't understand; I was appalled at defeats which I understood even less — for was not Sir Redvers Buller invincible?

And were not White and French and Baden-Powell mighty warriors before the Lord?

And I heard people lamenting — as Scotsmen will to this day — the death of Freddie Tait. It meant nothing to me then that this Freddie would never again pitch a golf-ball over the Swilcan or reach the fifth green at St. Andrews with two wooden club shots. I know now that he was typical of the gay and gallant youth who went out to Africa.

But in those days I only hated the villainous Botha the more, and the scoundrelly de Wet, and prayed every night that my nurse was wrong and that the "Black Krooger" wouldn't get me and that Cronje wasn't even at that moment in the suburban twilight, lurking in the tall artichokes, waiting to pounce.

And I remember the General Election when our candidate, Mr. Gibson Bowles, drove through the village behind a couple of spanking bays with his Party — our Party — my Party — colours fluttering bravely from the harness and from the whips and from the coachie's hat and from the candidate's lapel and from the four corners of the wagonette that he was in.

He — we — I — had stood solid for the prosecution of the war, for the knock-out blow, for down-with-the-pacifists, for the Union Jack, for the great and glorious Empire, and knocked our rival, our stinking, dirty cad of a rival into a whacking great cocked-hat.

And so at five years of age I was initiated into Europe's gospel of Hate.

Many years later I discovered to my astonishment, quite by chance, that the affair had been slightly different.

While I was being what the upper-middle-plutodemocrats call, for some reason, "educated," at an upper-middle-etc. school, I heard during my third or fourth year that the school possessed a library. Wondering idly if it contained some books and if not, what, I made some enquiries about its geographical position, and ultimately ran it to ground, — so to speak. (As a matter of fact, I had passed it at least ten times a day on my way to and from my "studies," and had occasionally decided to find out what it was. But up to that moment I had not done so.)

The Library turned out to contain quite a lot of books, and I turned to the shelf nearest to the door which was marked A. and flanked by marble busts of Samuel Smiles and Queen Adelaide.

There I found a whole row of books about the South African War and I read them all.

And what do you suppose it all turned out to have been — our hatred and our patriotism and our waving of the dear old flag and the deaths of many thousands of Freddie Taits in the gaiety of their youth?

It turned out to be a war for gold-mines and diamond-mines. It was a war to make the diamond-monopoly of the world safe for Cecil Rhodes and the inheritors of Barney Barnato, a Jewish acrobat from Houndsditch. It was a cruel, beastly war, fought against stubborn, slow, decent Dutch farmers by cruel, beastly methods. Thank God my Steward has the tact to stick to Holland's home war against the Spanish Inquisition and not go into the details of Holland's overseas war against the British Concentration Camps.

It was my first disillusion with dear old Europe. And then I discovered that the villainous Botha and the criminal Smuts had signed a treaty with Britain and had thus become automatically very decent chaps. And within a year of that discovery we were plunged into the World War and those two very decent chaps brought the whole weight of South Africa in on the side of Freedom against the modern Spartan Powers of Evil, and thus they automatically became Imperial Statesmen in the eyes — and amid high piping cries — of the pluto-democrats who had made the war against them fifteen years before, who had made millions and millions of money out of that War, and who had blackguarded the British Liberal Government which signed the Treaty with them.

Oh! Europa, you always loved bulls, didn't you? The strongest and the stupidest of animals. And your favourite child was called John Bull, after his father. And like his father, whenever he is in doubt, John rushes into the sea. There, at least, he is safe even if Spartans or women are upon his back.

My next encounter with Europe was that same World War. Well, I don't need to talk about that. We all know what happened. The upper-middles went hysterical over Mr. Lloyd George who had been anathema for taking the side of the Boers in 1900 and Iscariot for touching the pockets of the rich in 1909. The young men of the upper-middles went, with a few notable and still-unforgotten exceptions, to their deaths. The older ones who had attained high rank exchanged the lives of their men for C.M.G.'s and D.S.O.'s (letters which stand, though one would hardly believe it, for Distinguished Service Order).

The Empire's youth was thrown by incompetent polo-experts against uncut barbed wire, and France's youth was either mown down by German machine-gunners who had been tipped off the exact hour of the attack by Frenchmen from Paris, or else shot in cold blood by its own swines of senior officers.

You think I exaggerate, *ma petite*?

Believe me, I understate. No sensitive man or woman (if such a one exists) can read the real history of that war except in agony that such men could be.

Listen. Years after the War was over — and after War had been officially abolished for all time — the conscience of the French people began to creak uneasily in its sleep. Some men had been shot for cowardice during "the great years" and the widows and sisters and daughters and mothers were living in their villages and towns under the heart-breaking stigma of *mère du traître* or *veuve* or *sœur* or *fille*. Were all the cases true and well proved? Or had a little loss of head, a little partisanship — born, without any doubt, of an overwhelming love of the *Patrie* in the breasts of the senior officers concerned — crept into some of the courts-martial at which these men were condemned? And besides, there were a few survivors of the War knocking about, and they were telling some very queer stories in the *estaminets*, and the stories were beginning to circulate in a rather unpleasant manner.

So the French started what they called "Re-trials" of the dead men, and whew! What stuff came out!

This is what happened.

Years ago I happened to take an interest in those "Re-trials" as they were reported in the French paper, *Crapouillot*. I will tell you about one or two of them.

A middle-aged peasant in the French Infantry asked his corporal for a pair of cloth trousers because the winter of 1916 was cold (and by heavens it was cold, as I who froze in the mud of Courcelette on the Somme can tell and testify), and all his comrades were dressed in warm clothes, and he alone had a tattered cotton pair. The corporal gave him a pair of trousers that had just been pulled off a man who had been horribly killed by a shell. The man refused to put them on, and by the order of his Colonel he was shot for mutiny. At the court-martial the Colonel acted as prosecuting counsel and was also the judge. The peasant had no defender.

At a Re-trial in Metz a French Artillery officer gave evidence that his General on 7th March, 1915, had ordered the Artillery to fire at a trench full of French soldiers, because they hadn't succeeded in capturing the German trenches on the day before, at Souay in Champagne. The Artillery commander refused to fire at the French Infantry, and so the General compromised. He ordered four corporals, chosen at random from the Infantry regiment, and eighteen men, chosen at random, to go out into No-Man's-Land and cut the German barbed wire in daylight.

Any ex-soldier will tell you — no, that's nonsense, any ex-combatant-soldier will tell you, which is quite a different thing — that going out at night into No-Man's-Land was a very poor joke even on the quietest sector. Going out in the day-time was almost suicide, especially in Champagne. But these men went out into No-Man's-Land under heavy fire, lay in shell-holes all day, cut the German barbed wire at night, and came back. They were court-martialled for cowardice, and the four corporals were shot by orders of the General.

After the Re-trial a monument was erected to the memory of these four corporals at Sartilly in the Department of the Manche, but it was not unveiled by Monsieur Poincaré. Somehow or other, in his Sunday expeditions all over France to keep the militarist spirit alive, and to make another war possible, he forgot to go to Sartilly.

There was a French General who ordered a Company to attack against uncut barbed wire. They grumbled, but they attacked, and naturally were defeated, as anyone except a British General might have predicted when the wire was uncut. The General ordered that seventy-five men, taken at random, should be shot. His colleagues cut him down to twenty, and finally he declared himself content with six.

The men were not even tried. There was no court-martial. The counsel for the defence, who had not even been allowed to plead, protested with all the violence and sincerity that a compatriot of Monsieur de Voltaire can use when he is morally indignant. But it was all to no purpose. The matter had been reported to Papa Joffre, and Papa Joffre, that dear old man, ordered the men to be shot.

But nothing can compare with the appalling story of Lieutenant Herduin, Military Medal and *Croix de Guerre*, and Lieutenant Milan. At Verdun they stood a German bombardment of twenty-four hours, and then a German attack by two Bavarian Divisions and a Division of the Prussian Guard. The Lieutenants were the only officers surviving in their regiment, and with three hundred and fifty men they hung on. An order came through at three o'clock in the afternoon of 7th June, 1916, that they were to recapture the ground lost by their Division. At ten o'clock that night they had no more ammunition. The two Lieutenants, still surviving, by that time had only forty-two men left, and so they decided to fall back. And after five days of incessant bombardment and fighting, they marched back to Verdun with forty-two men. Their General had them shot for cowardice.

Lieutenant Herduin's widow lodged a charge of murder against the General, and the Minister of justice offered her a hundred thousand francs and admitted that her husband had been executed "by virtue of an erroneous application of the regulations." I need hardly add that the Minister of justice succeeded with ease in preventing the case being brought against the General. Perhaps they were at school together.

And statues decorate — if that is the right word — the European landscape — statues of Foch and Papa and Sarrail and Mangin. And they are called heroes.

This is not a grisly fantasia of Poe or Ambrose Bierce, nor is it an imaginative reconstruction of the mind of a typical German mass-murderer. It is the plain truth, as recorded in the annals of the Re-trials, as suppressed by every single French newspaper except the fearless *Crapouillot*, and as suppressed by every single British newspaper without exception.

Of course they were suppressed. Their publication would have struck a fierce blow at the infallibility of the upper-middles. And at that time — the 1925's and the 1926's — the uppermiddles were sitting on their money-bags with jellying posteriors and jerking pulses, more than ever cream-faced at the sinister advance of the Reds. Botha and Smuts were still Imperial Statesmen, but Mr. Lloyd George, having saved the Empire (including Botha and Smuts), had served his purpose and was by now sub-Iscariot.

So the upper-middles in Britain and France couldn't afford a scandal. So they suppressed the stories of the wholesale massacre of patriots by fellow-"patriots," and they continued to foster that elegant notion that Joffre really was a "Papa" to his men, that Mangin was a sublime hero because he had lost an arm, and that even Foch was a great soldier, and that anyway "the lower classes love being led by a sahib."

As a matter of fact, the lower classes, as they are called, do love being led by a sahib. The trouble is that the upper-middle-plutodemocracy has taken upon itself the responsibility of defining the word "sahib."

But while these dreadful crimes were being committed by the sahibs, the plutocrats were having a capital time. The French and the German and the British industrialists were passionately interested in the War. It's a story that can hardly be told without anguish. Up to the beginning of 1917 the Germans sent a quarter of a million tons of steel every month through Switzerland to the Comité des Forges in France. The payment for this steel was a certain amount of gold going through Switzerland, but it was also a promise that the French aeroplanes should not bomb the mines and the blast-furnaces and the rolling-mills in the Briey Basin, which the Germans had captured in 1914.

When General Sarrail, my Salonica chum, was commanding in Lorraine, he worked out a plan to destroy the Briey district. But Papa Joffre, dear Papa Joffre, to whom memorials are erected almost every week somewhere or other, heard about this plan, and summoned Sarrail to Paris where he had an interview with President Poincaré. And that was the end of the plan to destroy the Briey iron basin.

After the War Poincaré did more than any other human being to create a new war with his Sunday speeches at War memorials. He did as much as any man, even including Field-Marshal French, to prolong the War in which he did not fight, and in which Field-Marshal French could hardly be described as having fought.

But it was not an entirely one-sided arrangement. Germany sent to France magnetos for aeroplane motors, and France in return sent bauxite to Germany to help them to make their Zeppelins. Barbed wire played a big part on the Western Front, and a great deal of the barbed wire used by both sides was manufactured by the Drahtwerke of Opel and Company and had come to England through Holland. And Australia and the Straits Settlements and Ceylon and even Wales exported their products to Holland in vast quantities, and one cannot help suspecting that Holland did not use them all, but may have passed some on to Germany by way of payment for the wire.

I wouldn't dream of saying this to my Steward, who would bounce into Dutch anger if it was suggested that his country had helped the cause of Tyranny. But even Holland took its rake off between 194 and 1918.

. . . . .

I am rambling now, little one. But we are flying, and flying, and flying over the wine-coloured sea of the Hellenes, and there is nothing to do but to think and scribble. I suppose the patch of sea below us is historic. Half of history was fought out in Levantine waters, but we can't go into that now.

I'm only concerned at present with my farewell to Europe, and with what Europe has done to me, or for me, that I should thank her. "What's Hecuba to him or he to Hecuba, that he should weep for her?" etc.

That is an outline of how Europe's Hatred affected me — me personally. It was round me, almost imperceptibly, all the time from the days of Krooger to the Declaration of War in 1914. It then made me an obscure servant of its principles for five years, from the Declaration to the Peace Treaty.

For half a year I drilled, in order to learn how to kill Germans — and perhaps Austrians and Bulgars and Turks — and learnt the principles of artillery fire from dug-out fools who didn't understand the principles themselves; then for half a year I was set on by other dug-out fools — or by incompetent cowards who were either too frightened to go to the War or too stupid even to join the Staff — to teach the principles which I had learnt (by myself) to other poor children. By this time I had reached the age of nineteen years, and I lectured on ballistics, and gun-drill, and the mechanics of the gun, and the theory of telephonic communication, to lads of eighteen, nineteen, twenty — anything up to thirty-five.

But whatever the age, all, all were poor children, learning from me how to hate Bavarian and Westphalian and Saxon children with the best instrument which Vickers and Beardmore could devise for the throwing of an explosive shell, weighing eighteen pounds, three or four miles.

And I, who taught them, was nineteen years of age. The age of the Fresher at Magdalen, which I ought to have been; the age of the debutante of those days; two years too young to have legal rights; far too young then to have a vote.

Instead set down to drill a hundred men — all older than myself — and inspect their toothbrushes, and send them to prison, and give them leave to get married — God help them — and set down to instruct other officers in the art of gunnery.

That was my next half-year of Europe's charms. After that, the story becomes tedious. For I was caught up into close quarters with Europe's finest example, hitherto, of Hate, and it wasn't for a long while that I succeeded in running away from the Western Front in so neat a manner that I avoided being shot for cowardice.

But the time came at last when a gap appeared in the barbed wire entanglements of the back areas through which a civilian soldier could wriggle unobserved. The custodians of the gap had got careless. They had opened it so often for Regular officers who might be described — like the famous Babu — as Staff-hankerers, and for the younger sons of influential ladies, and for the gigolos of the mistresses of elderly Generals, that at last they didn't bother very much.

So I got through, and bolted for home, overtaking on my way several Portuguese.

Then came the end of the War, and I, like a hundred thousand other jaded, war-weary kids — I was twenty-three and felt like a hundred and forty — thought that the job had been well and truly done and that War was finished with for quite a while, and that International justice had a chance.

A good deal of the Treaty of Versailles gave us rather a shock. I don't mean the revisions of the frontiers. The frontiers of Europe — the old harridan's curves and contours — were a lot better after the Treaty than before. She got a sort of monkey-gland treatment at Versailles. But the Reparations stuff was clearly either crooked or lunatic. And we had had a definite hope that all our thousand friends hadn't died for crooks (we had long forgotten Freddie Tait, saps that we were) or lunatics.

So, as I say, this part of the Treaty gave us a shock.

But the shock was far out-balanced by the excitement that the first twenty-six clauses of the Treaty — of all the Peace Treaties — gave us.

For they were the Covenant of the League of Nations, and in the Covenant thousands of us saw a glimpse of the Land that we had toiled for in the wilderness. It was our Pisgah.

The clap-trap propagandists and unscrupulous politicians and dirty profiteers had screamed for four and a half years, "Kill them, heroes. Stab them, heroes. Twist their guts, heroes. It's the War to end War."

Whether we believed them or not, is neither here nor there.

But in the Covenant lay the possibility that those swine would be proved right in spite of themselves.

There was a chance, in the Covenant, that the scoundrels who profiteered and battened and careered and hid, during our years of fighting, might have turned out to have been Old Moore in person.

That was the next step in the history of Europe as I have known it.

The League of Nations — the one good thing that came out of the slaughter — the one piece of sanity in a maelstrom — the first modern notion that Sparta might yet be turned back by a modern Delian League.

Suddenly Peace found her Leaders, and they make as good a roll of names to the ear as the roll of Napoleon's Marshals, or Nelson's Captains, or even — shall we say? — Haig's Corps Commanders.

Wilson, Cecil, Nansen, Branting, Unden, Masaryk, Beneš, Henderson, Murray, Briand, Stresemann — these were the boys we fought our next campaign under.

We fought it as vehemently as we had fought our last campaign. I admit there wasn't quite so much danger, but there was even more enthusiasm. It was very satisfactory to direct the fire of a six-gun battery in such a way that Bavarian peasants were mown down in squads, and then to lengthen the range by a hundred yards or so to prevent stretcher-bearers coming to the help of the wounded (don't blame us. We were fighting Sparta with its own weapons, in order to end War).

But it was more satisfactory still to address a meeting of a couple of thousand people and get them wildly excited over the idea that the League was a workable, practical, simple method of putting into action the slogan which the crooks never intended should be put into action.

They had screamed, "War to end War," never dreaming of any other result than the bamboozling of children to Passchendaele or Mametz Wood.

We took their dishonest slogan and showed how it might, how it should, and, what's more, how it *could*, how it *could*, how it could, be brought to Truth.

The sea is blue beneath us still — I never quite understood that "wine-coloured" business of the Greeks. I wouldn't have described your eyes as "wine-coloured," unless perhaps, in their infinite mirror-like depth, they were holding a pair of mirrors up to your outsize claret-coloured friend (with the immeasurable and wheezy waistcoat). But that is neither here nor there.

At least, it isn't here. Thank God.

There is still nothing to do but to scribble. How is that wheezy waistcoat, by the way? Still wobbling pendulously in every zephyrous breeze that blows from the Riviera or from Harrogate?

Still enchanting you, with its mammoth curves? They find mammoths in Siberia, they tell me, very very old, preserved in ice, looking very odd, with no end of ivory in their heads, and without much hair. But I don't know about these things. The Greeks only called the sea claret-coloured. They had no mammoths — not physical ones, I mean.

I've forgotten what I was talking about. Oh yes.

League of Nations. Collective Security. That's where I'd got to in my discussion of Europa — the loony goddess.

We thought — we — the survivors of the latest in the long list of Armageddons — that Collective Security was the ticket.

And so we fought for it.

Once again we were subalterns in a war — a good war this time — I can't remember all the names, Gladstone Murray, flying-ace and hero of a thousand fantastic exploits, was one of the senior subalterns in our new army. So was Reggie Berkeley — dramatist, fast bowler, stout heart — dead, untimely, a few years ago —; another was Alan Thomas, who won all the medals, except the V.C., as a junior infantryman; Vernon Bartlett, who never gives up the fight; "Father" Cummings, grave, but always ready to laugh; Freshwater, still looking like Daddy Kruschen after performing incredible feats for years in the Line; "Jack" Hills, commander of a battalion at 48; Drury-Lowe, a Jutland admiral; Oliver Bell, huge, who found an aeroplane strong enough to carry him into the air so that he could attack the Hun; Forty, Stainton (whose hand-grip sent you automatically to an osteopath), Wyatt; Timmy Wood, small, tough, invincible, and hilarious machine-gunner; — heavens! how the names come back to me! — Boakes, Hester, and Hockham, the three ex-privates who manned our office-door as faithfully and as resolutely as they used to man a fire-step, or guard a sniper's-post — all of us were soldiers in the campaign to make the Covenant the thing that Woodrow Wilson and Robert Cecil and Smuts and Gilbert Murray intended it to be.

We had seen War, in one small way or another, so no one could say we were Pacifists or cowards. (I would like very much to see the man who told little Tim Wood that he was a coward. After two months I would take flowers to that man in hospital. It would be a waste of time to take them before because he would have been unconscious.)

. . . . . .

But we fought our new war even more vainly than the last one.

The Powers of Darkness, staggered for a race or two by the scintillating form of Woodrow Wilson's colt Idealism (by justice out of International Good-sense), soon rallied. The profiteers, the *embusqués*, the "hard-faced men" in the new Parliament, the land-owners, the rentiers, the upper-classes and their toadies, the reactionary Tories, both in England and in France, concentrated their energies on grooming and training their long-distance stayer Selfishness (by Self-esteem out of Self-interest), for the long race against the Wilson colt.

Also they mobilized an army of racecourse crooks — under the leadership of a famous gangster and hired saboteur, known in Apache circles near the Paris fortifications, as Poincaré — to use every dirty trick to nobble the brilliant Idealism which had already got away to a flying start.

What chance had we against cash and crooks? Idealism was duly nobbled. A few years later we substituted another magnificent animal sired by the Wilson horse, which we called Collective Security (by Idealism out of Practical Politics), and again the thugs got to work.

Every Friday the thugs lined up openly at the tradesmen's entrance of certain ducal and marchesal and baronial and financial and journalistic and political mansions for their pay-envelope, and they certainly gave service for their fees. No killer for Capone, or Bugs Moran, or Johnny Torrio or Dion O'Banion, or the Genna brothers, or the Aiellos, ever did more conscientious and efficient work for their employers than the toadies did for the upper-classes, and the upper-classes, in turn toadies, for the Big Shots above them.

You see, my precious, we were attacking Vested Interests all the time. Not that an Interest which is Vested is necessarily bad. Far from it. Society as we know it couldn't live without them. But we were attacking the bad ones, and the bad ones are always the Capones, the dangerous ones, the employers of killers. We were out to destroy the power of the gun-makers — those jolly fellows I was telling you about who gladly sell barbed wire and shells to each other from opposite sides in a war; we were out to destroy the traffic in drugs, and the traffic in women and children; sweated labour in factories; foul conditions in ships; and above all we were out to destroy War.

With a whoop the thugs came down and destroyed us. They did it, roughly speaking, on these lines: it was hammered into the heads of the populace, by every available long-distance method, not that the League was bad — oh no — but that Wilson is an American: and you know what Yankees are, *my dear*; that Cecil is an idealist: and you can't trust *idealists*, the poor sweets; that Nansen is divine: *darling*, what a he-man, but so bewildered, the pet, just a tool; Branting, Unden, Beneš: well, they're just foreigners; Henderson? A Red, if ever there was a Red: paid by the Kremlin: in roubles: gold roubles: stamped with the hammer and sickle; Gilbert Murray — well — dammit — he's a Greek scholar, or something, *and* a vegetarian, *and* anti-blood-sports, oh to hell with him; and Briand is a frog, and Stresemann is a Hun. So there you are.

And, my dear, think of the expense of it. Why, Great Britain alone has to pay a hundred thousand pounds a year to support all these Reds and frogs and wops and dagoes in luxury, and in *what* luxury, my dear, in great marble palaces on the Lake of Geneva, where they never do any work except intrigue against our great and glorious Empire.

Those were the approved lines of Thuggee, and they succeeded beyond all expectation.

Collective Security was shot to pieces by Boss Baldwin's strong-arm squad of men and women.

It is recorded that when Dion O'Banion was shot to pieces by Capone's men in his own florist's shop, he was buried in a silver coffin under a pyramid of flowers which had been brought to the cemetery in twenty-six lorries. Not least conspicuous among the floral tributes (a technical term much in use in provincial newspapers) was a huge basket of orchids labelled simply, touchingly, movingly, "From Al."

Few things have moved me more than Boss Baldwin's verbal tributes to the League of Nations, after it had been mown down by his pals between the years 1931 and 1936. And few baskets of orchids have been more gaily colourful and more freely sprinkled with tears, than the one which bore the black-edged card, "From Stan."

I assure you, my ex-divinity, my *ci-devant Reine du Monde*, that this isn't really an exaggeration.

That is — in essence — how the Tories set out to destroy the League — our League, the League that we really believed was going to bring into practical, world politics the vague, funny, half-formed ideas that we had fought for, and which almost all our friends had died for.

We were kids most of us — so no wonder our ideas were vague and half-formed — and the men and women who set out to destroy the League were much older and much more experienced in the ways of the world. Of course they had more to lose than we had — they their money-bags, we only our lives — and so perhaps they fought more tenaciously for their treasure than, I think, our generation did for ours.

I don't know. We fought pretty well, but we were out-gunned, and it is munitions which win nowadays.

I don't suppose for an instant that you will read all this long venomous snake of a letter, and it doesn't really matter to me whether you read it or not. But I must get Europe's poison out of my system on the same sunny afternoon that I am getting Europe herself out. All, all, is to be left behind. The new world is to be faced as if it was a new life. The skin of the snake is to be sloughed off, and chucked into the Mediterranean as we come to Alexandria.

So whether you read or not, I'm slogging on. You can always bequeath the manuscript to the British Museum, to be opened on the day, about twenty-five years hence, when the Elgin Marbles have been finally cleaned away into smoky Pentelican dust, or you can use it to light fires with, or to make into spills for lighting cigarettes which touch your lips — no I didn't mean that. I can't even remember what your lips look like — or you can tear it into small pieces and use it for a paper-chase — with you as the twisting, subtle hare, and all those fools and knaves and cowards and rogues as the clumsy, Benedictine-laden hounds.

In short, what you do about it is of no concern. For myself, I write.

Between those years, 1931-1936, the politicians who represent pluto-democracy fired blast after blast from their sawn-off shot-guns into the League of Nations, so that at last it crumpled up, went all bow-legged, and came down to the ground, just like Dion O'Banion. And everything in the florist's shop was pretty except the twisted, shot-sprinkled body of the florist.

But there was a big wreath "From Stan" on the silver coffin.

. . . . . .

So these politicians killed our League and our notion of Collective Security amid the highpitched adoration of the Union of Women's Conservative Associations.

What happens?

We accept the inevitable. Our ideal of Collective Security has been smashed as if it was a web of thistledown at the slow mercy of that great black slug which we call in Scotland a horny-golloch. Very well. We retire into obscurity and wait.

Meanwhile the politicians have substituted their own method of conducting international affairs. For years they have screamed that our methods must inevitably lead to a war, but that they will eat their hats if theirs does not inevitably lead to a lasting peace.

Within about a year their new policy had failed with the most resounding, reverberating Bang in the annals of modern history, and that goes for something, my snippet, believe me. There have been some pretty dainty failures in diplomacy and policy in the near past, but this one was the biggest of all. It was the crackerjack.

But — and here we reach the phantasmagorical climax — those same politicians were magnificently resilient. They bounced once or twice, and then popped up again, admitting their crashing failure, and announced that they had a brand-new policy, once again which would inevitably save Britain and maintain Peace in Our Time.

Naturally we are a little surprised when it turns out that this brand-new idea is Collective Security. But we are not so much surprised when we are told that just in case the politicians haven't got time to create a new League of Nations before another war can burst on us, it would be esteemed a great kindness if we will all step out pretty smartly into the defence forces of the country.

The Greeks had their world, and anything beyond it was beyond the Streams of Ocean.

This situation is beyond my Streams of Ocean to comprehend.

Let me put as lucidly as I can for your little brain behind that Correggio face of yours — damn, that's set me off again —

> If one could have that little head of hers
> Painted upon a background of pale gold
> Such as the Tuskan's early art prefers!

Well, I will admit that there was a time when I used to think quite a lot of that poem of Bob's, in the old days when I was on the chain-gang. I would even go further and say that Gaffer Browning in that very same poem wrote a description of a woman's face that might have been written about you, with you sitting disdainful on the model's platform, and the Gaffer gazing at you with one passionate eye and the other on the entrance by which Elizabeth Barrett Browning might pop in from time to time, intentionally, to see that there were no goings on.

Elizabeth B. Browning's dog was called Fluff, but that girl herself was no bit of fluff, believe me. The lines I mean in Bob's poem, which might have been written about you who are so beautiful, are:

> Then her little neck, three fingers might surround
> How it should waver on the pale gold ground
> Up to the fruit-shaped, perfect chin it rounds.

I am perfectly prepared to swear in front of Rhadamanthus, Peter, Minos, and all the famous judges, that you are a hell-hound. But not all the Torquemadas will make me say that your chin isn't perfect.

But I won't deny that there were times, long ago, as long ago indeed as last Tuesday fortnight, when I wouldn't have minded two particles if I had put three fingers round your little neck, and squeezed it so hard that I would have landed on the drop, with a Sheriff and a parson beside me.

But I didn't. So why should I boast about what I would have done if I had had the chance, when a fortnight ago I had the chance and I didn't do anything, except fly?

I've forgotten what I was writing about. Oh yes. I was going to put my position, *vis-à-vis* the politicians, and the financiers, and the newspaper-owners, and the pluty-democracy:

(1) I, a child, fight for Freedom. 1914-1918.
(2) The boys are busy in Whitehall and the City of London, doing very nicely, thank-you. 1914-1918.
(3) I survive and want a nice League of Nations so that I won't have to fight again.
(4) The boys say the League of Nations gives them a pain in the neck, and they've got a rasper of an alternative which consists of destroying the League so that we will have Peace for Ever. We won't ever again have to censor letters from Alf to Eliza which end up, "Hopping you are in the Pink as it leaves me at present, Yours, Alf." and with the underside of the flap of

84

the envelope marked, cabalistically, S.W.A.K. Which, after all, only means Sealed with a Kiss. A sweet and moving message from the fighting-man who doesn't know what he's fighting for, to his girl, who doesn't know what he's fighting for. Perhaps both feel vaguely that in their heart of hearts he is going out to fight the Spartans to defend his girl from them. I don't know. It's possible.

(5) The scene shifts to the Egyptian Hall. Herr Devant and Signor Maskelini invite a spectator to join them on the platform, to see for himself that everything is all square and above board.

(6) The spectator joins the two *maestros*, and the new policy suddenly vanishes.

(7) The boys rush out of the Hall and shout for help. "We must have Collective Security," they roar, "and everybody must be ready to die for the principle of international decency and honour." And there is a stupendous roll of cheering from the rows upon rows of Tory women, and reactionary grafters, and political careerists.

(8) I, and a hundred thousand others who fought in the War of 1914-1918, go off and enlist in one form of National Service or another. And that is the story.

So we are preparing for a war which, had decent, honest, idealistic, practical, clear-sighted men and women been in office, could have easily been avoided; a war that is being forced upon us by a policy that we have loathed for twenty years; a war that would have been impossible if the Tory mind had not been so desperately set upon its money-bags; a war that might even now be staved off if the Tory Machine had not been so determined that the rich, half-witted son of an "important" half-witted landlord or pseudo-nobleman or plutocrat was more fitted to solve problems which he didn't understand than a brilliant man of the ordinary people who did understand, but who had no money.

So the Tory women — in the intervals of screaming that men ought to be flogged — and the grafters and the careerists and the fools have danced round their ancient totem-pole so resolutely and so vigorously that they have danced me, and those like me, out of Europe.

As a matter of fact it is the women's dance which controls ultimately the fate of the soldiers. Sir Jebusa Spillikins would not be able to cast his vote in the House of Commons, with four hundred other J. Spillikins's, for the totem-pole, if it was not for the incessant toil of Lady Spillikins in the constituency.

It is Lady Spillikins who patronizes the villagers so sublimely that their proletarian back-bones wriggle with ecstasy; it is Lady S. who pats the babies and cuts the wages and distributes gingerbread at Christmas and vamps the Socialist Mayor by dancing a D'Alberts with him at the Annual Gala of the British Legion.

It is upon Lady S.'s broad bosom that Sir Jebusa, and the totem-pole, and flogging for men, and the Party rest assured. And it is on those ample curves that everything that I have stood for, everything that I have longed for, everything that I have instinctively prayed for to the Unknown God, have fallen in a handful of powder for Boreas to laugh at and whisk away into the Sahara.

> And the men that were boys when I was a boy
> Shall sit and drink with me.

That must now be rewritten. "And the men that were soldiers when I was a soldier, must come and fight with me."

O Zeus, what an eternal ass you were when you became a Bull and brought Europa to Crete. Why couldn't you have been content to be a Swan or a Shower of Gold. Leda never did me any harm, nor did Danaë. Leda only produced Castor and Pollux — the first heavy-weight boxing-champion of the world — in the direct line of Jem Belcher, Peter Jackson, Jack Johnson, Dempsey, and Tunney. Castor and Pollux were a pair of tough eggs if ever there were two. But then what else could Leda expect but eggs? But they never worried me, Zeus. They were decent chaps.

And Perseus never did me any harm.

But Europa! O Zeus, you did a bad job of work there.

So I say farewell to Europa with all my heart. To Crete the strumpet went. And Cape Ampelousa, on the corner of Crete, is my last glimpse of her.

And lastly, my sweet little Europa, there comes back to me a dim recollection of my Greek dictionary, of a heavenly word which is written down in the dictionary as meaning "bullmaiden: *i.e.* Europa."

Bull-maiden and loony-goddess. What a girl.

. . . . .

Alexandria is in sight, so I must stop this philosophical treatise.

I can see the coast of Egypt. And here and now I flatly refuse to say a single word about Cleopatra. So don't get the notion that I'm going to compare you to that relentless lovely.

If you have got as far as this, pray accept my felicitations on your endurance.

If you haven't — well, there it is.

Good-bye, sweet. The further I sail, the safer I am, and so, academically, the sweeter you become. R.

P.S. — But don't get ideas into your head. It would only be a waste of time.

11th April, 1939
Over the Sea to Palestine

I meant to stay in Alexandria for several days and even take the time to drop down the Nile to Cairo and Assuan and Luxor. It's true I never had any ambition to look at the Pyramids, which have always seemed to me one of the most tedious forms of architecture in the world. And they were built by slave-labour anyway, which isn't likely to endear them to me.

All your life depends upon slave-labour, doesn't it? And it was to escape from it that I am flying. There isn't any difference between the Pyramids and your small existence within the Mayfair square mile. Both are built on the same Institution.

And the Sphinx must be a bit of a bore from all accounts. Whenever I hear of a mysterious smile like the Mona Lisa, or the Sphinx, or those film-actresses who bob up from time to time and are technically called "enigmatic," then I am always pretty certain that I am up against a sweet simpleton who only smiles like that because she can't think of anything else to do.

Sphinx, Mona Lisa, you, all are the same with your enigmatic smiles. Your smiles, those little ones, so mysterious, seeming to be so unfathomably profound and wise, seeming to be so understanding, so tolerant, drive ordinary men to distraction.

But they only drive me, who am no ordinary, bamboozled man, to the South Sea Islands. I'm not deceived. The Sphinx and the rest of you riff-raff have no secret.

Except the secret of Power over fools. You smile, and fools grovel.

But you smile to me, and I fly scornfully to the Islands of Lodore. That's the sort of chap I am.

.   .   .   .   .   .

But all the same I would have liked to have seen the Valley of the Tombs of the Kings, and the view over the Desert, and all the places which are, roughly speaking, hallowed by the very jolly decent exploits of Beau Geste.

But it was not to be. Circumstances ran against me. In fact, they ran against me so toughly that I am all of a tremble still. I can hardly hold my pencil in my hand, although my great machine is reeling off its three miles a minute as steadily as a swan paddling upon a Suffolk bywater.

I'll tell you all about it.

In my hotel in Alexandria I met that fellow, whose name I can't remember, who used to dangle round you last year. I was bowling along to the bar, full of *bonhomie* and good cheer, and I bumped into him. What the devil was his name? You would know in a moment, simply by telling your maid to look him up in the card-index of adorers.

Anyway, his name doesn't matter. Nor does he, really.

He was that politician-chap, with brown teeth, who is always in office because he knows exactly when to turn his coat, and God knows from the sartorial angle it always needed turning, what with its shiny elbows and all, and how to make himself pleasant to the people who are going to prefer the new aspect of his veteran suiting.

He came up to me, of course, in the most matey style, which he wouldn't have done if he had known that I am never coming back to England. But obviously the first thought that crossed his mind was, "Here's a chap who might be useful to me in London," and the proof of this is that he stood me a couple of drinks in no time. You remember that he was never very forthcoming with drinks when he couldn't see any immediate return on his outlay.

He was out in Egypt, he told me, at some length, on a tour of inspection for his Ministry. That lad will climb high, if only because he gets so much practice in climbing. But he told me over the second drink that he was going back to London tomorrow, and immediately I fell into a panic. If that miserable slug goes back to London tomorrow, I said to myself, he will inevitably have the nerve, which all slugs have got, to telephone to you and ask you, you, the Queen of the World — I mean the lady who used to be the Queen of the World, in old days, long past, and long forgotten — out to dinner: And in the course of his stuttering conversation on the telephone, he will tell you that he met me in Alexandria, and the velveteen paws will be out again, stretching sleekly over an escaping mouse.

But by Heavens I'm an *escaping* mouse. Escaping is the operative word.

So I listened to a two-hours description of the work of this rat's Ministry, all spoken in that vague monologue, with lots of meaningless gestures, which all junior Ministers seem to affect when they want to conceal their nincompoopery. And then I sneaked away to make all preparations for skipping out of Alexandria in time.

It's a bore. But I can't take any risk at this stage. I have got without mishap as far as Alexandria, and eastwards from here I have a much better chance of safety. It was this first part of the journey that was worrying me. I don't think even you will stretch out a claw east of Suez. At least, not very far. At least, I hope not. At least — well, anyway, I'm taking as few chances as possible.

Yesterday evening I spent wandering in the town. It was my first real glimpse of the East. I have never even seen a palm tree before. The old mansions on the outskirts of the town are rather beautiful, coloured in blue and pink and creamy yellow, and all very, very dusty. But in the suburb in which I walked, these old houses, which had once obviously been sort of minor palaces, have fallen upon evil times. One may be a dilapidated warehouse; another may be an obscure little factory; a third may be full of goats; and a fourth may be deserted altogether. Beyond them was the Harbour with the massive old forts at the entrance, and most of the British Mediterranean Fleet lying at anchor.

I went into a café and watched the be-fezzed men playing dice and dominoes, and eating mysterious things out of greasy pits of paper, and smoking those long, curling pipes. But the clatter of the talk, and the dominoes, and the smell of the clients and, in fact, the appearance of the clients, were all too much for me, and I swallowed a glass of warmish beer and fled.

This morning we started early and flew along Aboukir Bay, where Nelson's Fleet performed that extraordinary manoeuvre of getting inside the French Fleet as it lay anchored in the roadstead. It was a perfect example of the Nelson touch as practised by Nelson himself (but not, as I've already said, by some of his successors). He came sailing along with a following wind, towards evening, on the chance of finding the French Fleet. When the look-out man on the leading ship shouted that he saw the French, there wasn't the slightest hesitation. There was no question of waiting until the next day, although the evening was coming on. Nelson went straight ahead, and as he got near the French he saw by the length of the French cables that there was room to get between them and the shore, and he brought off the great manoeuvre.

But the great manoeuvre was a possibility that had been discussed a score of times in the Admiral's cabin during the evening conferences, and although it was brought off at full speed, almost at a moment's notice, it was the product of long and intricate study.

The sound of the explosion of the huge battleship, L' Orient, in that Bay down below and the glare of the explosion against the night — for it blew up at about 10 o'clock — told General Bonaparte far away across the desert to the south that something was very much wrong with his ships.

Then we crossed the Delta of the Nile, which is an amazing sight. First of all we came to neat little squares of cultivation, most of them yellow and a few of them green, and then mud and sand and long stretches of stagnant pool, and then the streams of the Nile twisting down into the sea through the mud, and complete emptiness as far as. the eye could see towards Cairo. I suppose there was some cultivation, but I couldn't see it. It looked just like a lot of deserted streams.

The Suez Canal was infinitely small, and a P & O mail-boat which had just emerged was a toy, as we went seawards again for the run to Lydda, the first halting-place in Palestine.

The Wireless Officer has just reported mysterious Morse Code callings. It comes back to me, in an agony of apprehension, that a Sunday newspaper published a huge photograph of you just before I left with a story underneath it, "She is learning Morse Code." And an interviewer in the same paper reported you as saying, "You never know when it might come in useful."

I wouldn't put it past you to be putting Morse Code at this very moment on to my lovely charter aeroplane.

Not to attract me. That wouldn't be your exquisitely subtle method. You wouldn't be so clumsy as to try to get into touch with me. But I'm terrified of your slant-wise ways. And if I catch the Wireless Operator giving a surreptitious message to the Captain, I shall sack the lot and send them all back to Amsterdam and wire for a new crew from Siam or Tangier or somewhere.

But surely I can trust my Dutchmen. They are quiet and solid and slow and unbelievably efficient. Will my Captain, a burly young man who thinks of nothing but weight, and petrol gauges, and weather reports, be distracted by a tapped-out message of endearment from a little snip some thousands of miles away?

I refuse to believe it. My Captain is of the stuff that sailed up the Thames with a broom at his mast-head, and collared a world-monopoly of quinine. He, a strong, sensible youth, who can land an immense aeroplane at eighty miles an hour as delicately as a butterfly edges down upon a gossamer thread in August, he isn't going to take his mind off his job for you and all your blandishments.

So tap out your seductive messages. Go on. Tap them out. We don't care. We are men, up here, and we know it.

. . . . . .

What are you doing now, I wonder? I've got all muddled with the change of clock from Greenwich time to whatever time we are in now. Are you getting into a taxi after the theatre and stretching out the loveliest of all legs on to the seat in front of you? Or are you yawning in bed at noon over a cup of chocolate, and beginning to irradiate heaven on the telephone to other men as once you used to irradiate heaven to me? Or are you cutting six appointments to run off to the hospital where a girl to whom you are devoted is ill?

I will say this for you. Women loved you too. I wonder why. No, I don't really. You could so easily have hurt them, but you never did. You could have flaunted your deadly power in front of them, but you were scrupulously honest and never did.

In the worst moments of the last three years when I had to talk to some woman about you or explode, I never found a woman who was not on your side — damn them. They all seemed to think that it was I who was behaving badly to you, by being wild and irritating and unbalanced and crazy and emotional, and that you were behaving sweetly to me by being so soft and understanding and forgiving.

They were fools, of course. No one but a fool could take so grotesquely wrong a view of a situation between a man and a woman.

But that isn't the point. The point is that they really believed that to be the truth, and they couldn't have believed that if they hadn't loved you.

You *did* visit girls in nursing homes. (It used to infuriate me as a waste of time.) You did have women who were devoted to you. And I suppose there were occasional — very occasional — moments when it might have been suggested that I was slightly wild and a trifle unbalanced, and even possibly a trifle irritating from time to time, at long intervals.

But then if you hadn't had one or two redeeming features in your character, I wouldn't have been in love with you.

And, incidentally, it proves how utterly out of love with you I am now, that I can so dispassionately set down some praise of you. It has all become so impersonal.

.   .   .   .   .

The low, sandy shore of Palestine steals through the shimmer and then a great dark blob of country obliterates the sand. It is the dark green of evergreen trees in clear sunshine. In Poland, years ago — heavens! how many years ago — the sunshine was not so clear and the Bialowieza Forest was blue in the distance, and in Russia, when the winter sun was pouring down upon the snowfields, the forests were black. But these orange orchards are deep green, where the Jews with toil and sweat have recreated Jaffa and invented Tel-Aviv.

Twenty years ago, my Wireless Operator told me (though he could only have got it second-hand because he looks about twenty years old himself) the whole country was sand where now the oranges grow and the dark green of fertility is steadily pushing the burning silver back and back.

I'm going to land at Lydda to get some petrol and have lunch. R.

Dot, dash, dash, dot, dot, damn that wireless. I feel uneasy. Dot, dot, dash. . . .

Same day
Lydda

A neat little airport, concreted and well-laid-out, with excellent beer and the largest oranges I've ever seen in my life.

Lydda is the home-town, so to speak, of St. George of England. It was here that he was martyred, and it was here that Richard Coeur de Lion built a church for him and so made him the Patron Saint of the English.

He's had an interesting career, has George. He was, after all, only a non-commissioned officer in the Roman armies, but he's managed in sixteen hundred years to pinch the legend of Perseus who rescued Andromeda near Lydda; he's got himself mixed up in Mahomedan minds with Elijah; and he got his Dragon from Dagon, the Philistine rival of Jehovah. The only real set-back which George had in his long and illustrious career was when Mr. Gibbon attacked him and had the nerve to pretend that he was a fraudulent bacon-contractor from Asia Minor. George was a sergeant, not a quartermaster-sergeant. That ass Gibbon didn't know the difference.

. . . . .

I'm surprised that there are so few soldiers, but probably they are hidden away all round us. I can see a faint outline of Haifa, the terminus of the crucial pipe-line from the oil-fields, but I can't actually hear the explosion of bombs or the rattle of revolver-fire.

It's been a pretty business — this Palestine Mandate, hasn't it?

All three parties in the wrong — British, Jews, and Arabs — in one way and another.

Britain is in the wrong because she can only defend her Eastern Empire by keeping her Mediterranean route open and, in order to do that, she must control the Haifa pipe-lines, and, in order to do that, she must maintain her control of Palestine, and yet she will go on protesting that she is only actuated by the highest and most idealistic motives.

The Jews are in the wrong because they have gradually persuaded the world to believe that Mr. Balfour promised them Palestine, whereas he actually promised them a National Home in Palestine, a very different thing.

And the Arabs are in the wrong because Britain, and Britain alone, at colossal expense of lives and money, with heroism and with suffering, freed them from the centuries-old domination of the Turks and founded four independent Arab states, Yemen, Hejaz, Iraq and Saudi Arabia. Without British soldiers, the Arabs would not be free in those four states to-day, and yet they do not hesitate to murder British soldiers to try to get control of a fifth state to which they have a very doubtful — to put it mildly — claim.

It's all jolly fine for the Arabs to scream about T. E. Lawrence and how nobly they behaved in helping the British against the Turks. They were simply doing nothing else but taking a very small part in an enormous effort to help them. And as for the MacMahon correspondence on which they base their claims, no one has yet been able to understand exactly what that well-intentioned soldier actually did promise them.

And it's all jolly fine for the Jews to get together and chant extracts from the psalms about their right hands forgetting their cunning. For twelve hundred years they weren't able by themselves to rescue Jerusalem from the Saracens, and it wasn't until General Allenby did it for them in 1918 that Palestine was at last open to them.

It's all a muddle, of course, but it would be a help if two of the three parties who have made mistakes would be a little more matey with the third party who has also made mistakes. And that's all I am going to say about that.

We're off again, across Mount Ephraim, and a desolate sinister country it is. Mount Carmel is looming in a shimmer away in the north. "Pharaoh is but a rumour, do they say? As I live, saith the Lord, surely like Tabor among the mountains, and like Carmel by the sea, shall he come!"

There's a goodish bit of history down below us, with such things as Deborah's palm-tree and Naboth's vineyard and the Gates of Jezreel. If I could only identify them, I would be able to see where Gideon brought off his celebrated night attack, and the ground where Elisha and Ahab and Judith and Holofernes walked. It is a country of rocks and deep valleys with a little greenness and a great deal of dust. There are scrubby little trees here and there, and in front of us another range of dry, barren hills by Gilgal and Shiloh and the wilderness of Bethaven.

All this country was the northern frontier between Judaea and Samaria, the No-Man's-Land, and like all oriental frontiers it was a place of raids and battles and sieges and massacres, and to judge from its appearance from the air, it looks exactly the place for grim and horrible deeds.

Benjamin was the tribe of these parts, and don't get the idea that, because "Benjie" is a term of endearment nowadays, the tribe of Benjamin were pleasant fellows. — They ravened like a wolf, you may remember. Jeremiah wrote about the bloodshed and the slaughter. "A voice is heard in Ramah, lamentation and bitter weeping, Rachael weeping for her children: she refuseth to be comforted for her children, because they are not."

It is a country for men on foot, fighting in ambushes and from behind rocks. There are very few chariots in the Bible in this part of the world, and Jehu, the son of Nimshi, learnt nothing of his furious driving down there.

Mount Hermon has just appeared covered with snow, high above the clouds, far away beyond Carmel, but I can't see any of the cedar trees of Lebanon.

We climb and climb over Ephraim until the long, blue hills come out on the horizon, and there at last is Jerusalem and the Fords of Jordan beyond.

The Captain comes and asks me if I want to go down and look more closely at Jerusalem. There is a nice following wind apparently, and we have plenty of time on our hands, even for the long haul across the Syrian desert to Basra. So we are dropping and circling over the City.

It's exactly as you would expect it to be. The Mount of Olives, the Brook Kedron, dry in the heat, the Mosque of Omar, the inner wall and the outer wall, the pale yellow roofs of the old town and the smart red tiles of the new, they're all there, just like the framed mezzotints which hang on the walls of half the Nonconformist cottages of England.

The old town inside the main wall is tiny, and this isn't an optical delusion, because we're now circling at a couple of thousand feet.

History isn't made in the New Yorks and the Buenos Aires and the Bombays and the Greater Londons and the Moscows. History is made inside Jerusalem's walls, and in little places like Athens, and Rome, and Valley Forge, and Runnymede.

In the whole of recorded history how few men there have been who have changed the course of history. Of how few can it be said, "If he hadn't lived, the world would have been a different place." Christ, perhaps Mahomet, certainly Charlemagne, Caesar, Napoleon, Lenin, I can't think of any others at the moment. And so it is with places.

Athens, Rome, and Jerusalem, and Mecca are key-points in the human story. Four out of all the myriad dwelling-places of mankind.

And now, bless my soul, if that isn't Jericho, "the City of Palm Trees," where the balsam came from, and where the climate is so sultry that the men couldn't stand clothes made of anything except linen, and whose walls fell down in sheer terror at the noise of Joshua's trumpetry. Jerusalem is perched on its rocky, dusty hills. Jericho is down in the watery, sultry valley. And hillmen have been from time immemorial too strong for the plainsmen — always with the exception, the inexplicable exception, of the Romans, who lived on the edge of the marshes of the Campagna and were ready to take on all comers at any weight, in any style, Queensberry Rules, or catch-as-catch-can, or all-in, or New York's No Foul.

But in Palestine only the hill-men survived, and Jericho's walls were knocked down for an old song — so to speak.

And here's the Jordan, surely the most unimpressive trickle that ever attained everlasting fame.

The Jordan Valley is a strange sight. At first it looks as if the river is very broad and very green, and then you realize that the broad green stripe is vegetation and that the river itself is very small and very muddy. Little tributaries run down into it through salty swamps and jungly thorn-bushes. It's a bit wider in flood-time, my Second Pilot tells me, and it reminds me that the Old Testament calls the floods the Pride of Jordan. "Though in a land of peace thou be secure, how wilt thou do in the Pride of Jordan? He shall come up like a lion from the Pride of Jordan." There used to be lions in this jungle, and even now, I believe, there are wild beasts hiding among the thorns — wild boars and leopards and wolves. Isaiah wrote, "The land of trouble and anguish, whence are the young lion and the old lion, the viper and fiery flying serpent."

And that hill on our right, on the other side of the Dead Sea must be Pisgah, and a nasty, rocky-looking place it is too. The Lord was in an unforgiving mood when he made an old man, one hundred and twenty years old, climb Pisgah to see the land which he wasn't going to be allowed to enter. But the Lord was an uncertain factor, even in those days, continually, "popping out from behind rocks in Sinai" as Logan Pearsall Smith has pointed out somewhere, "wearing a very large beard."

The Dead Sea is wonderfully green, which is clever of it considering the amount of muddy silt which the Jordan drives down into it. In fact I think the Dead Sea is the greenest patch of water I've come across yet, except the lake in Provence near the Mont de la Sainte Victoire which is called the Barrage Zola. That is dark jade, without a faintest tinge of blue. The Dead Sea looks as if it might turn blueish, dimly, tentatively, if the Jordan would only cooperate with some nice, pure, snow-soft water from Lebanon, if it would, as it were, come clean. But the Barrage Zola is immutable, like Envy, or the emerald, or the laurel.

Climbing again now, to cross the mountains of Transjordania, the land of the Ammonites, and to catch our fast tail-wind that is going to bowl us along into Mesopotamia.

.   .   .   .   .

I'm fairly plunging into Asia. At two hundred mph and sixteen thousand feet in the sky. I am racing into an unknown world, and I feel that I am free of you at last, for ever and finally. You've lost your last chance, little one.

I don't even wonder what you're doing at this moment. I've no more interest in you. It's three o'clock on a Saturday afternoon, and by Greenwich time you'll be sitting in a restaurant choosing your luncheon and terrifying your pathetic ass of a cavalier by your knowledge of the intricacies of cookery, and of the subtleties of the wine list.

Did you ever meet a man — in all your hundreds — who did not pull his waistcoat down and send for the wine-waiter and try to impress you with his unfathomable expertness in the hocks and the clarets? And did any one of them not perspire gently down the side of his nose when it gradually emerged that you knew rather more than he about wine and vastly more about food? There are two places where the man ought to be allowed — even if only out of Samaritan gentleness — to feel that he is a God. One of those is at the restaurant table when he has the wine list in his hand; the other is in bed.

But you've got no tact. At least not at the restaurant table. (And I fly to the east because I don't know the answer to the second.) You will be making your cavalier look remarkably unlike the dominating men who made the word "cavalier" with their curveting horses and their cavalry charges and their swaggering chivalry.

But what do I care?

Who lies beneath your spell?

as the Indian love-lyric plaintively enquires. As if it matters a row of pins to me. I only know two things, that someone new by this time lies beneath your spell, and that he's a poor fish.

What are you saying to him? With what slow, dark looks are you fastening him to the chain? And with what infinite contempt will you glance at him when the last rivet is serenely dropped into place and yet another fool falls into step with the other fools who march round and round their kennels, and honestly believe that they're enjoying themselves?

It's a desert below us now and no mistake. At first Transjordania had some villages, and patches of cultivated land checkered the red-brown hillsides. We passed Amman, the crucial town on the Transjordan railway that Colonel Lawrence aimed at so long and so, in the end, successfully, and we crossed over the thread of the railway itself.

The railway is the last trace of the West that I shall be seeing for an hour or two. Wherever there is a railway there is always a reminiscence of my fellow-countryman who put a spoon against the nozzle of a kettle and deduced, thence, somehow, the irresistible power of steam-pressure. (Just as Isaac Newton cried, when the apple fell off young Master Tell's head, "It fell at the rate of thirty-two feet a second, and that must be the Force of Gravity," or was it something like that? Anyway, it's near enough.)

And where there is a railway there is always a link with that other fellow-countryman of mine who took the spoon and the kettle and converted them into Puffing Billy, and the cow, and the exhibits in the Science Museum at South Kensington (the English having characteristically appropriated the Scottish inventions, just as a few years ago they appropriated the Scottish railways as well).

But after we had left behind us the Transjordanian thread of legacy from Watt and Stephenson, we went straight back to the ancient method of transport — the most ancient of all methods — the transport of the desert world.

In three minutes — in the most modern of transport-machines, my huge Californian Douglas aeroplane — I went from Stephenson to camels and donkeys.

The railway vanished. The caravans came out. I could see them plodding along. The days of Moses and Joshua were still alive. The land of Burton and Doughty and Manasseh hadn't changed.

And here is an interesting thing. In the far-off days when I too fought against the Spartan-HunPrussian attempt to jump in heavy boots upon free laughter and gay clowns — and helped to down it, we used to study unendingly the photographs which our aviators took of the trenches and back-areas of the savages.

And one thing we noticed — and when I say "we" I mean the amateur soldiers, not the professional soldiers who seldom noticed anything except dirty buttons or an unmathematical alignment of horse-pickets, or a streak of grime on a whitewashed horse-line post — where was I? Oh yes. One thing we amateurs noticed was that Spartan-Hun savages are, in some ways, the same as anyone else. When there was a hill to cross, or a sky-line to walk over, they, naturally, preferred to dodge round by valleys or sunken roads, and it was only at the very last conceivable moment that they crept quickly out and made a dash across the open. There is nothing surprising about it. We did it ourselves. Every man in danger has always done it. It is human nature. It is animal nature. Read Maeterlinck's description of the white ant, and you will have a description of any soldier. Hide when you can, run when you can, and only come into the open when you must.

Now, by a study of our aeroplane-photographs my amateur major and I deduced the habits of the German army from the tracks which the photographs revealed. We knew, being human beings, that there was a reason for every track, because all of them had been made by human beings like ourselves. And so, in every sector in which the amateur major and his amateur subaltern fought, it only took a few days for us to make a complete picture of the life of the German troops against us.

And we fired our eighteen-pounder guns accordingly.

And so it is in the Transjordanian desert.

The ground is scarred and scored with tracks. At first you think they are natural marks on the ground, but after a bit you realize that there is a reason for each one.

You realize that not one of them is natural, that they are the immemorial pathways of immemorial camels, plodding, plodding, and still plodding.

And then the scene becomes, instantly, fascinating. Because it becomes a game. You are flying over the brown, reddish-brown, grey-brown, light-brown, deadly dark-brown, of the Syrian desert, and all the time there are the tracks. What is the reason for this track or that? Why does that one curve round right-handed and come back again, and why does that one drift away left-handed over the edge of the slopes? Why do they part company and join and part company? The answer to these questions is simple, after a few minutes' thought, to anyone who has studied aeroplane-photographs as my major and I did, so long and so earnestly. The four things which the camel-caravans, from the earliest times, ten thousand years before Moses stood upon Pisgah, must have wanted, must of course have wanted, were these:

(1) Shade, if such a thing existed.

(2) A route that was not everlastingly cluttered up by other caravans.

(3) The shortest route, after allowing for (1) and (2) and above all

(4) Water.

With those four principles in mind, one can understand the varying and twisting tracks of Transjordania. The caravaneers took, from all eternity, the shady side of the hills; they separated here and there, to get away from each other's too-well-known conversation and also on the chance that they might find, on a by-pass, something to eat that the others would miss; they didn't go so far off the main route as to make them lose a great deal of time; and, incomparably the most important of all, they concentrated at the end of the day's march upon water.

So I look down and I see the Bedouin spider-threads on the brown land, each thread creeping away from all the rest and stealing away, hither and thither, apparently for no reason, aimlessly. But I look down again — after the short interval when my Steward brought me a bottle of Dutch beer, acquired mysteriously in Palestine — and I see the spider's web of tracks converging and converging and I know that if I look two miles ahead I shall see a patch of green among the arid desolation.

Where the tracks converge, there will be water, and the visible sign of water is greenery.

Has it ever occurred to you — what an infernally silly question — has anything ever occurred to you except the art of bewitchery, you lovely Medea of our times — that the Old Testament is full of references to water, and streams, and pools, and springs, and wells?

We are leaving behind us the rich country. I can still see Gilead by craning my neck over my left shoulder, Gilead, the place of the famous balm, whence came "a company of Ishmaelites with their camels bearing spicery and balm and myrrh, going to carry it down to Egypt," and the valleys which are full of pomegranates and apricots, of olives and wheat and vineyards. At least I am told that the valleys are full of the delectable foods. But I can't see anything but the green strips of cultivation among the barren hill-sides.

But cultivation is falling behind us, and in front of us is the bleak land of the cattle-owner, cattle being a general name in this case for camels and sheep and goats and cows. This is, literally; the land of the Bull of Bashan. This is the end of growing and the beginning of hazardous pasturing. It is the divide between the fat farmer and the hungry nomad. And as soon as the farmer got over-fat — every fifty years or so down the ages — the hungry nomad burst across the divide and set civilization back once again for another fifty years.

When Reuben was wondering whether to cross Jordan and have a dart at the Canaanites (into whose hand the Lord had characteristically sold the Israelites), Deborah worked herself up into a hysterical rant (she must have been a sort of Aimée Semple Macpherson, just a sweet home girl) and screamed, sarcastic-like:

> By the water-courses of Reuben great were the resolves!
> Why did'st thou abide among the sheep-hurdles?
> To listen to the bleating of the flocks?

There you have exactly the situation: Reuben, dwelling on the edge of the cattle country, and depending for his life on his water-courses, is being tempted to make a foray into the agricultural land. (I don't have to waste time and space in pointing out that he is being tempted — nay! goaded — by a woman — his little pet — to do this dastardly thing.)

It appears to be a small point, but it is of infinite importance to world history, this division between the cattle and the crops in Transjordania, this division between the hungry fighting-man on a camel and the intelligent agriculturalist who studies the rotation of crops and the seasons of the moon.

The position to-day is precisely what it was in the days of Joshua. The waves of nomadic, Arabic hunger are ravening round the orange-groves of Jaffa and Tel-Aviv for precisely the same reasons that Midian swarmed across Jordan and pitched their sinister black tents in the Vale of Jezreel and the Plain of Esdraelon, until at last they were hammered by Gideon.

It is the Desert against the Market. The Sands against the Farmer. The Camel against the Corn. Only the Romans, in all recorded history, were able to draw a frontier-line against the Desert and hold it inflexibly for centuries. But then the Romans in their prime were men of iron, and they sharpened their swords to keep the Peace and uphold the Law.

I remember a thing George Adam Smith — scholar, parson, and wit — once said about this very same land. He had visited Transjordania — on foot — and he had come to the site of Pella, where once was a town with a castle and temples and colonnades and all the material and social dignity of a Roman provincial city. He found nothing but a few ruined basements and a few columns, and — and this is the point — the tents of a Bedouin tribe. That is what he said, as near as I can remember: "Frail houses of hair, they were here five thousand years ago, ere civilization spread from the Nile to the Euphrates, and they flowed in again upon the decay of one of its most powerful bulwarks. For the Arabs have been like the ocean, barred for a time, yet prevailing at last over the patience and virtue of great empires."

And this, the Arab infiltration of fighting barbarism, is what the English Empire, with its lack of patience and only a certain amount of virtue, is facing today.

At this very moment Britain is grappling in Palestine with this identical problem — how to save the progressive, cultured, peaceful, Jewish orange-groves from the hosts of Midian.

Will the camel-driver triumph over the land of Drake and Milton? I wonder. He has stout friends, little Dr. Goebbels, for instance, and the men who poured their Duce's mustard-gas upon the descendants of the Queen of Sheba, and the little yellow poison-ants of the Pacific, and now the black men of Morocco, under that most Christian gentleman, the mutineer Franco.

They're a queer crew, these pals of the camel-driver, but they all join in one thing. They hate Freedom. They hate Liberty. They hate truth and decency and love. But shall the camel-drivers win to all eternity?

Must Dark Ages always come out of Mongolia and Scythia and Berlin and the Desert to burn the libraries of Alexandria, and torture the Pastor Niemöllers, and stamp upon the beautiful things which man has slowly and laboriously created through centuries of sweat? It's a grim thought if we are to believe that Christ is always to create his Anti-Christ and that no oasis, no spring of pure water, no marble colonnade will ever be safe from the Desert, and that the everlasting answer to Woodrow Wilson's Covenant is a victorious Hitler.

We have crossed the railway and now we are purring out over the desert and I can see a few of the Midianites and their slouching camels, and here and there a crowd of goats and sheep, and little clusters of "frail houses of hair," black, which were here five thousand years ago and which have outlasted the whitest and hardest of marble.

The greenery is steadily being extinguished by the relentless dust, and the tracks are converging more and more closely as the springs and water-pools grow more scarce. The land is getting dark, for there is more rock than sand and the rock throws a shadow in the afternoon sun.

And now we pick up Britain's imperial artery, the vein on which depends ultimately her lands between Gibraltar and Singapore, the great Mosul–Haifa Pipe-Line.

It's only a tenuous line across the desert, but it's the key to a great many doors. It runs straight — the Romans themselves would have been proud of its straightness — for miles and miles and miles. I suppose it dips into nullahs and swerves round hillocks. But one can't tell from here. From here it is straight. It is Euclid's ideal. It is the shortest distance between two given points. Though perhaps one ought to say two taken points. I suppose no one actually gave us Haifa or the Mosul oil-fields. I fancy we just went and took them.

It's a remarkable sensation, flying over the Pipe-Line. I depend, for my life, upon the petrol and oil which the Dutch authorities provide for me in my handsome charter-'plane. If it wasn't for the petrol and oil I would tumble on my nose in a most unpleasant fashion. And below me is the oil on which the Mediterranean Fleet depends. And within an inch of us, on each side, are the camels of five thousand years ago. They have defeated the Legions and the marble cities. Will they also defeat the Pipe-Line? They, the animal-riders, destroyed the chariot, and the ox-wagon, and the bullock-cart, everything which ran upon wheels. Now they are encroaching again, with their bombs and their secret assassinations — the first assassins came out of the Desert, the sons of Hassan, and they took his practice and added his name to it, in all filial piety, so that the Sons of Hassan became Assassins — and now I will start again.

The nomads are encroaching upon the railways of Syria. They ambush a train and they blow up a station. Anything on wheels is anathema to an Arab. Anything, in effect, which moves faster than the camel.

So what about the aeroplane?

Will the five thousand years of savagery extend for another year or two? Will the black hair tents ultimately combine to destroy the Pipe-Line and bring one more empire crashing down into white dust?

We are balanced upon a precarious knife-edge of filigree. Our system of what we delight to call civilization is almost at the mercy of strolling Bedouins. We buy oil-wells, and we build refineries, and we clamp down a pipe across a thousand miles of sand, and we heap up great battleships, and we feed the battleships on the oil which comes across the sand from the wells — and all the time the Desert is watching.

The Desert has seen Moses come, and Joshua, and Richard of England, Saladin and Guy de Lusignan, and General Bonaparte, and Allenby, and is the Desert any weaker or less tenacious than it was, all that time ago?

Once it was a matter of saving wheeled transport on the roads. Then it was a matter of saving rail transport. And now it is a matter of saving the Pipe-Line.

The first instant that Britain relaxes her Roman rôle of maintaining order in the Syrian Desert, then she starts to go down the imperial decline.

. . . .

There is an occasional pumping-station on the Line, a nest of green roofs, and silvery tanks in a rectangular stockade, and an aerodrome, and they look just about the loneliest places in the world. They aren't really lonely — in the physical sense — for the nomads are creeping amid the sandhills round them, watching and watching, and two or three times a day the aeroplanes go past on their way, the fortunate ones, to the outer streams of Ocean and the Islands of Atlantis, and on their way, the miserable ones, to Mayfair and the streets at the back of the BBC. But in the real sense of the word those pumping-stations must be desperately lonely.

The desert is becoming less rocky and more sandy, and so the colour is lighter. I don't know if the change is for the better. The rocks made it dark and sinister; the sand makes it dry and dusty and thirsty. The rocks seemed to threaten interlopers. The sand seems to stretch out to absorb waters that belong to other people. This is the immemorial desert, cruel and menacing and shining. We have left behind us the last vestige of green and now it is all yellow. The tracks are fewer and fewer. Even the camel-nomads have been daunted by the endless parchment of windfurrowed slopes.

Only the Pipe-Line marches on, the symbol of the West with its internal-combustion engines and its battleships.

Somehow it is a comforting sight.

Heaven knows I'm done with the West for ever, and I sincerely trust I'm done with battleships for ever. But that flow of oil is one of the things which are defending Freedom in its last stand against the new Dark Ages, and so it has my blessing — which must be a great comfort to the shareholders and directors of the Iraq Petroleum Company.

But even the best of friends must part, must part, as the old song says, and now the captain has put two alternatives before me with his devastating Dutch clarity and simplicity. Either we follow the Pipe and finish up this evening in some frightful spot near Mosul, where the mosquitoes outnumber the beer bottles by a considerable margin, or else we part company and strike away right-handed and spend the night in extreme splendour in the new airport hotel — at Basra.

At this moment the Steward joins anxiously in the discussion and hints that the bar of the new hotel is fitted throughout with chromium and plate-glass, and that the barman leaps to and fro from bottle to bottle with an agility that was hardly paralleled even by the Spanish Infantry after the heroic Netherlanders cut the dykes and introduced aquatic sports for the first time into European military history. I haven't got it in my heart to sing to him the poem which Sir John Squire wrote after a brief, but quite long enough for Sir John Squire, visit to the Hotel King David in Jerusalem. The song began,

> Jerusalem the chromium, with gin and orange mixed,

but the anguish on the Steward's face is so harrowing that I simply haven't the heart. Besides the young pink Wireless Operator has laid down his head-phones — so you can chuck your Morse Code for a few minutes — and, his face drawn and haggard, is trying to tell me that Amsterdam has just wirelessed a storm-warning. It appears, according to the pink youth, that a tornado of unheard-of tempestuosity is raging at Mosul, and that, so far from an aeroplane surviving, it is extremely unlikely that a strong man could push a wheelbarrow through it without being bowled over.

It is a beautiful report, completely in accord with the Dutch lucidity to which I'm getting accustomed, and it would terrify me out of my wits if the aeroplane hadn't got a looking-glass just behind the Wireless Operator's stance in which I could see the Steward silently and appreciatively clapping, and even the Captain loosing a slow wink.

Of course I am overwhelmed by the weight of public opinion. We leave the Pipe-Line and make for Basra.

After all, there is something to be said for a brass-rail and a barman who leaps to and fro. It will take me back to the International Club in Geneva where Leon used to leap and mix, while Vernon Bartlett cried, "*Joli à voir,*" in the days when we tried to make a new world and still thought that Youth must triumph in the end and that Love must defeat Hatred.

What simple little chaps we were! We know better now.

Yet — I wonder. I still wonder occasionally, tough old scarred cynic that I am.

There was once a man called Blackie, a Latin professor who also knew a goodish bit of Greek. As Blackie lay dying, his greatest pupil, his best-loved pupil, by this time a flour-miller in the north of Scotland, went to say good-bye to the Master.

Blackie awoke for a moment and recognized him and took him by the hand and murmured, ἀληθεύων ἐν ἀγάπῃ "Speaking the truth in love, in love, do you hear?"

Was he right? Can it, will it conquer in the long last?

In the dim distant years — it must be at least a week ago now — when I used to live in the South West One district of London, there was a strange little madman who used to come down my street once in a while. He was mad, of course. Everybody said so, and what everybody says is always true.

Well, this little madman was about seventy years of age and he was deadly poor. His clothes were almost rags and his boots — they were an unmatched pair — were in holes, and his shirt was of the vintage of last Tuesday fortnight. He pushed in front of him a little cart, laden with all the sort of thing that isn't of the faintest use to anybody in any circumstances, old bicycle tyres, and the ribs of umbrellas long-exhausted, and mudguards of destroyed Fords, and segments of false teeth, and ladies' hats of 1910, and lithographs of the Prince Consort in Saxe-Coburg tartan, and antlers, and broken bird-cages.

So far as I ever saw, he made no attempt to sell any of these assorted goods to the populace. He pushed his cart and he pushed it and he pattered after it, and he didn't give a damn for the populace.

But — and this is the whole point of this digression — there were two things about the little shabby fellow which made him the blood-brother of Professor Blackie.

The first was that he wore a silk hat — on top of all his careless shabbiness — yes — a real honest-to-God silk hat — which was exactly the same as Blackie loving Greek on top of all his Latin, and which is exactly the same as a man wearing a buttonhole, or a woman taking infinite pains over her step-ins when she is only going out to dine with some other woman. It is, as Wilde so rightly pointed out, *an attitude to life*. A topper to a hawker (who doesn't hawk) is the same as Greek to a Latin professor, and the same as silken delicacies which will not be seen by a lover.

And the second way in which this Antolycus of Pimlico, this snapper-up of useless junk, resembled Blackie was that he eternally chanted through the streets, in a high, musical voice:

> Beautiful Love,
> Beautiful Love,
> Beautiful Love for all.

Of course, the little be-toppered man who hadn't washed for months was a bigger man than I shall ever be. His words were "Beautiful Love for all." All.

I haven't got Love for all. I've had in my time a very great deal of beautiful hatred for lots of things and lots of people, Bloody Hitler and Benito, to start with a nice couple, and the clowns who took you to the Savoy and the crooks who invited you to Paris, and the politician with the brown teeth whom I ran into in Alexandria.

And just think of all the other things which I've timidly disliked in the past, and which I would still think badly of if I wasn't now tranquilly happy in a new life. I certainly can't claim the silk-hatted pedlar's universal benevolence, but not even my worst enemy could maintain that I any longer feel Hatred for anything. When I bravely left you, and your small smile, and your twinkling wit, and those most beautiful of all blue eyes, I left Hatred behind as well as Love.

Besides, in my palm-fringed, lagooned, coral-island I won't have anything to hate.

Except that I reserve the right to loathe the men you are talking to today, and all the stinking vices and follies and selfishness of civilization. I won't ever be using my rapier again with which I've pinked so many humbugs and liars, but I'm going to keep it clean and polished and sharp in case — just remotely in case — any swine come to my island.

In a way I'm sad that I won't be in the forefront of the skirmish any more against the hellhounds of darkness. I had a good time. I won't deny it.

But one can't have everything in this benighted world. And to escape from loving you I've got to give up hating cruelty and Conservativism and crooks and clowns — if indeed any distinction can be drawn between any of the four — which is sad but just can't be helped.

One of the noblest scenes in modern literature is when Cyrano is dying and he imagines that, he is surrounded by all his lifelong enemies. He draws his sword and attacks the shadows:

> *Que dites-vous? . . . c'est inutile? . . . Je le sais.*
> *Mais on ne se bat pas dans l'espoir du succès.*
> *Non, non. C'est bien plus beau lorsque c'est inutile.*
> *Qu'est ce que c'est que tous ceux-là? Vous etes mille?*
> *Ah! je vous reconnais, tous mes vieux ennemis.*
> *Le Mensonge! Tiens, tiens! Ha! La! les Compromis.*
> *Les Préjugés, les Lâchetés! . . .*
> *Que je pactise?*
> *Jamais, jamais! — Ah! te voilà, toi, la Sottise!*
> *Je sais bien qu'à la fin vous me mettrez à bas;*
> *N'importe: je me bats! Je me bats! Je me bats!*

Lies, Compromise, Prejudice, Cowardice, Stupidity, how I hate you all! No, I don't mean that. I mean, how I have hated you all in the past. For me now the palm-fringe and the coral.

But all the same, I still think that the dingy hawker of unwanted mudguards was a better man under the stars than Cyrano or I.

Though, what comes of it, after all, what comes of "Beautiful Love for All"? What about it? Is it any good? Or must we fly for all eternity to the coral seas of oblivion?

I tried loving you and it wasn't any good. You preferred supper at Claridge's with a clown, or lunching at Hurlingham with a crook. I thought — silly juggins — that the busted little devil in the topper was right. I alone thought that he wasn't mad, but that of all people he was sane. But it seems that I'm wrong once again, in the company of Blackie.

"Speaking the truth in love, in love, do you hear?" is what I tried to do. But there! Clowns and crooks are more amusing. Or are they in the long run? Or are they? Well, you'll find out some day if anyone ever does. And then perhaps you'll tell me. Just put a notice about it in the Agony Column of the *Gardens-of-the Hesperides Gazette*. The nymphs will call my attention to it in the intervals of dancing round the Golden Apple trees, and I shall be dancing with them, platonically.

The sands are not quite so fiercely white now and here and there is a patch of green and even a pool or two. The desert is almost finished and we are coming to the edge of Mesopotamy.

There are streams now and cultivated ground, and there are the clear aquamarine waters of Lake Hamaniyeh with lots of black tents on its banks, and marshes and irrigation-canals, and flocks of sheep, and horses, the first since Alexandria, and the muddy Tigris on the left and the blue Euphrates in front.

Baghdad in a moment, so I'll stop scribbling to examine the romantic city of the Caliphs. R

Beautiful Love for All, huh?

Telegram handed in at Baghdad at 4 P.M., Same Day

City of Caliphs very like you stop All glamour gone stop just a pain in neck stop Infinitely prefer Southend Pier on August Bank-holiday, with Gaiety chorus to the pair of you stop Have a nice time stop Give my love to anyone who asks for me stop Collect on delivery R

Same Day
Basra

The Steward was right. The barman here springs about like a demented monkey behind his chromium barricade, but he is very far from being demented when he starts assembling the ingredients of a White Lady (and there's an ironical name if ever there was one. The colour is white, like you all. But it's a black business, like you all). He can knock you up a life-saver in as brisk a style as ever I saw, and that goes for Leon too. If only Vernon Bartlett were here, the bar would be echoing with the stirring cry of far-off days. "*joli àà voir, joli à voir.*"

After we left the old metrop. of Haroun-Al-Raschid in disgust and a great hurry — as per cable C.O.D. — we sailed down the place which is so often called "the cradle of civilization." It is doubtful if it was a cradle, and it certainly isn't civilization, but let that pass.

As for Baghdad, it may have been all right at one time, but it isn't now. I can't remember what poet wrote (but I suspect that chap Flecker)

Is not Baghdad the beautiful, oh say!

And I answer without hesitation, "Was, maybe. Is, no," and it's the only possible answer. So let's leave it.

The first thing to watch for after Baghdad is the Arch of Ctesiphon, but it looks too small from the air to be as impressive as it ought to be. It's in a loop of the Tigris and obviously there must have been a large city there once, to judge from the excavations which are going on all round the Arch.

But from the air its main interest is that it brings us once more into the zone of that damned World War. For it was at Ctesiphon that General Townsend made his lunatic attempt to capture Baghdad and was heavily defeated by the Turks, as anybody could have told him that he would be.

Townsend's men were heroes, and they deserved something better than Mr. Townsend. After months of marching and fighting in a ghastly climate, and under a still more ghastly administration from the Indian Army High Command, which would have drawn some sharp words from Miss Nightingale, who understood these things, the men were thrown into a forlorn battle so that Mr. Townsend should have the credit of capturing Baghdad. They failed, and were marched back to a town which I'll be seeing soon, a town with an even more dreadful legend than Ctesiphon.

I suppose I ought to have run across and had a look at the mounds which are all that is left of Babylon, but I just couldn't be bothered. Any one mound looks pretty much like any other mound, and I'll be able to sentimentalize over "Babylon, Babylon is fallen," just as easily from the warm, coral beaches I'm making for without the bother of actually going to have a look at the place. So I thought I'd save petrol (though Heaven knows I'm so rich that a few hundred gallons of Shell are nothing to me) and, still more important, save my Steward and Wireless Operator a little anguish, and cut out the mounds of Babylon.

So I gave orders to a delighted crew that we'd push on down the Tigris at maximum speed. The Captain sprang at his controls and opened up every throttle, or whatever they're called; Sparks grabbed his earphones to tell Basra that we were arriving at a rate of knots; the Second Pilot shoved away his portfolio of Rembrandt reproductions and busied himself with maps; and the Steward brought me a bottle of beer without being asked, and said that gentlemen like me would never meet Philip of Spain in afterlife. William of Orange, he hinted, as he poured, was pretty nearly the only gentleman in my class.

Everything was gay as we spun along the fertile land between the rivers, Tigris on the left, Euphrates on the right, and the Garden of Eden beneath.

And then the gaiety died away from me. From my crew, no. From me, yes. They were Dutchmen whose wars for Freedom were successful a long while since. They didn't know what that white-roofed town in the bend of the Tigris meant to people who had been compelled to fight for Freedom not so long ago.

That white town by the river was Kut-el-Amara, to which Townsend led back his heroes after Ctesiphon, and in which he, with some small help from them, was beleaguered by the Turks. They had marched in the heat, and fought, and suffered, and now were to be starved.

In the end Townsend had to surrender: his men could do no more. After the surrender the captured army was divided by the Turkish captors into two parts. One part consisted of the entire garrison, save one, and it was marched by the Turks in indescribable circumstances into the deep interior of Asia Minor, hundreds and hundreds of miles, to a prison camp at Afion Karahissar.

The details of that march are too dreadful for any words, so I won't write any words about it. And if you ever meet one of the few survivors, don't speak to him about it. That march was one of the horrors of the world.

The other part of the garrison consisted of one man — General Townsend himself — and he was treated by the Turks as an honoured guest and imprisoned in a charming house on an island in the Bosphorus, or somewhere thereabouts.

Anyway, wherever it was, the gallant General was treated in a genteel fashion by his Mongolian jailers. His men were not.

And when, later on, he became a Member of Parliament, he went back to Turkey and dropped a visiting-card on his pals who had done him so proud.

That is why the sight of Kut-el-Amara gives me the shudders. It gives me the creeps — the fighting, and the heroism, and the starvation, and the tortures, and Afion Karahissar, and the genteel prison somewhere near the Bosphorus.

But we were moving at our maximum speed by that time, and at two hundred and twenty miles an hour it is possible to lay even General Townsend over one's shoulder in a few minutes.

So we bundled over the vast mud flats and marshes of the Tigris and came to our chromiumplated anchor in a sea of delectable gin-bottles.

The local Leon has been too much for me. I'm going to bed.

No. On second thoughts, no.

> Whether in Babylon or in Baghdad, life runs out.
> Whether with sweet or with bitter wine the cup runs out.
> Drink, drink, for under this Earth there will be no drinking,
> There will be everlasting sleep without wine.

So long as the sleep really is sleep, and really is everlasting, I suppose the absence of wine won't matter so much. But if there turns out to be a flaw in the staff work, then the prospect is grim indeed. So I think I will take Omar's tip and sneak back to the chromium dervish for a final quick one. R.

Jolie d àvoir. I used to think that you were pretty to watch. You are still. But not by me.

12th April, 1939
Twelve Thousand Feet Above Mohammerah

I woke early this morning to the thunder of the engines of an Imperial Airways flying-boat which was taking off from the river on the homeward flight, and as the dawn was coming I got up and went out for a stroll.

The river's got the oddish name of Shatt-el-Arab, and it's really simply the combined Tigris and Euphrates. They join a little higher up for the last swirl down to the Persian Gulf. Another white flying-boat was moored on the water, and on the far bank a row of palms was reflected darkly in the river as the sky behind them grew pearly and dappled with the dawn. It was all very quiet and cool.

After breakfast I went down to the town itself to buy a topee and become thereby a genuine honest-to-God-Britisher-in-the-East, and sat in a shop in a native bazaar while agitated shopmen tried to find one that would have the everlasting honour of fitting the Great Lord of the West, the Pride and Glory of the British, i.e. the holder of a pound sterling.

The search went on. All the topees were too small. Rivals in trade were anxiously mobilized — even though it obviously involved profit-splitting, always a repugnant thing to the man who has done the actual hooking of the fish — but all to no purpose. Every one was too small.

So I left the sorrowing bazaar, pushed my way through the mob of screaming children, and went for a walk in the town, through narrow streets with closely over-hanging gabled houses, down to the canals which carry the barges and small boats through fringes of oleander to the Shatt-el-Arab and the Gulf.

But the sun was high by this time and I was feeling particularly a fool in my black felt hat from St. James's Street.

Two-thirds of the populace thought that I was just an ordinary English maniac. Half of the rest paid no attention to me whatsoever, and the other half of the rest thought that I was Mr. Eden in person.

So, for all those three reasons — and I still can't decide in my mind which was the most influential — I fled from the laughter and the coldness and the adulation back to my car and drove through the dusty palm-trees, past the mud huts, and along the deeply-dug waterways, out of Basra to the hotel.

It was only a step from the hotel to my aeroplane and, after a final visit to the bounding barman for a final Basra pick-me-up, I hid my black hat under my arm and nipped under the midday sun into my 'plane.

Once again we taxied to the end of the aerodrome; once again we wheeled slowly round to face the wind; once again the 'plane quivered like a war-horse snorting at the nostrils, and we were off.

We were off down the delta of the two great rivers, and now within a few minutes here I am, over the oil-refineries of Mohammerah, so short a distance is it, when you are flying at two hundred miles an hour, between Nebuchadnezzar and John D. Rockefeller — or between Belshazzar and Sir Henry Deterding — I get confused between the various empires of those days and these.

But what I'm trying to say is this: it took me two hours to leave the Pipe-Line and get back into the ancient domain of the camel and the black tent: it has taken me a quarter of an hour to leave the oleander-sprinkled canals of Basra and return to civilization as we know it, in the open fires, the heavy smoke, and the rows and rows of shining oil-tanks at the Mohammerah Refineries.

So closely nowadays does the West harry the East.

Not for nothing, perhaps, has the West studied the legends of the East. When Ali Baba wished to destroy the Forty Thieves, he poured oil upon their heads as they crouched in jars. Now the West saves the modern Ali Baba from perpetrating so dreadful a crime by taking all his oil away from him and shipping it into tankers and sending it to Singapore to defend the British Empire against Japan, or, alternatively, and without prejudice, sending it to Japan to enable Japan to attack the British Empire.

It doesn't seem to matter which, so long as Ali Baba, the original inhabitant, doesn't get any of it.

The only point left to be decided is: out of the Arabian, or Irakian, or Persian, owners of the oil, and out of the British, or American, or Dutch, concessionaires, and out of the bondholders, and preference share-holders, and ordinary share-holders — who, who — I ask you — who are the modern Forty Thieves? Whoever they are, Oil has fallen upon their heads, not to destroy them as in Ali Baba's day, but to enrich them and theirs for ever and ever, or at any rate for two generations.

At eleven-thirty this morning I was having a final snifter with my chromium-ensconced barman; at eleven-forty-five I was crossing the eternal Delta of the Mesopotamy rivers; at twelve noon I was smelling all the dirty smells of the Texas and Oklahoma oil-wells.

It was with a feeling of relief that I left both the Delta and the Devil behind me, and fetched out over the Persian Gulf.

I was glad to have escaped for a while from the everlasting contrast between a life that is pastoral and agricultural and a life that is smoky and efficient.

The oil-wells came too suddenly after the palm-trees. It gave me a jolt. It was too abrupt a transition from ancient to modern. The camel-rider may ultimately bring the Desert back to the shores of the Mediterranean, but he may find that the oil-magnate has forestalled him and has destroyed the world even more quickly. Over the long sand of Transjordania I had seen the motive power of mankind's beginnings, which is food and drink for animals; over Mohammerah I am looking down at the motive power for what may well be mankind's ending, the fuel for bombing aeroplanes.

With which depressing thought I will now leave you and engage the Second Pilot in a discussion upon the finer edges, so to speak, of ice-hockey, a pastime to which he is much addicted in the Dutch winters.

If you're a very good girl I may drop you a line from Karachi. R.

Did you know that the Garden of Eden was in Mesopotamia? There was another sweet girl for you.

Same Day
Karachi

I have had a terrifying experience since I last wrote. In fact it was not until a nice large dinner was safely stowed away that my nerve returned and it was possible to sit down and write to you about the Persian coast.

Whew!

What a sight!

I have seen in my day the plains of Asiatic Russia, in mid-winter, with the temperature sixty-seven degrees of frost and a wild wind blowing; I have seen a German barrage of heavy shells come down so thick round me that they were elbowing each other for room to pitch; I have been buried; I have walked at midnight from one coach to another in a European express-train a fraction of a second before the train broke in half and left me standing on the very edge of death; I have been bitten by a louse and waited five days to see if it was a typhus-louse; I have seen a pair of deep blue eyes — the most beautiful that ever were seen in all the thousand corners of the world — in a great rage because their worshipper had remembered to say how exquisite they were, and so they had been deprived of a legitimate reason to be in a great rage.

But of all these terrifying things I don't think I've ever seen anything so terrifying as the coast of Persia — except, perhaps, the deep blue eyes.

For hundreds and hundreds of miles we flew along the edge of the Persian Gulf.

The sea below us was serene and smooth, marred here and there by an occasional oil tanker from those refineries, and redeemed by white-sailed fishing-boats which were not a day younger than a myriad years.

The Captain of the 'plane was cheerful because he'd got a following wind. The Wireless Operator was cheerful because he had sent a message — at my expense of course — to his girl in Rotterdam. The Second Pilot was deep in a book on Van Cuyp. The Engineer had oiled his engines so thoroughly that he felt it safe to take a nap and leave the Captain in charge, and the Steward was in high spirits because he had changed some Italian money into Indian rupees with the leaping bar-tender and had diddled the bar-tender in the transaction out of the equivalent — in some vague currency or other — of eightpence halfpenny.

These Dutch! They are superb. They will give you the moon, provided that it doesn't belong to them; and they will insist on three farthings if they are sure that they do belong to them.

Never mind. They are supremely efficient. Their beer is good. Their pictures are good. And their ideas of Freedom are on a par with mine.

But, in spite of all this cheerfulness and satisfaction on board, I couldn't take my eyes off the Persian coast.

As far as the eye could reach, to the farthest limits of the horizon, rose range after range of mountains, for all those hundreds of miles, parallel with each other and with the seaboard. All were the same colour, light grey with cold, steely blue shadows, and all were bare rock. There was not a patch of colour, not a tree, not a house, nothing but these vast serrated ramparts, split and scored and fissured with a million clefts, nothing but cold, cruel, hard desolation.

Even the desert was not so remote, so awful, as this blue-white terror. For the desert did have an occasional pool or string of camels. But here was nothing, absolutely nothing. The words came into my mind that Captain Scott wrote in his log-book when he reached the South Pole and looked round him and cried in agony, "Great God! This is an awful place." I could feel a little of what he meant. If only one could see *something* which had life in it, or something, say a ruined house or a deserted village, which had been connected with life, however long ago, it would have saved one from the feeling of desolation which is so unspeakably frightening.

And the colour was so cold. If it had been reddish or black or purple, it would have been less menacing. But the light grey of the rock and the ice-blue of the shadows made me think of a snake that is waiting, motionless, for the unwary passer-by who may come within reach of death.

If there was even a single tree in sight, it would make the vast solitude just faintly bearable. There would be just that difference between the possibility and impossibility of life.

But there is no tree — not one — upon the grim, cold ranges of Dashtistan and Laristan, and I can gain no comfort from my map which tells me that behind them lies Shiraz, city of wine and roses and the poet Hafiz. I can only see that silent, blue-white-grey eternity of high jagged edges.

And as if that was not enough fun and games for one day, I had to land at a God-forsaken, filthy spot called Jask, in order to pick up petrol.

Jask is the low-water mark up-to-date. A spit of red-hot sand runs out into the Persian Gulf; it is separated from the foothills and the wilderness below those mountains by a row of seedy palm-trees which look as if very large mice had been nibbling at them for a very long time; on the end of the spit is a clump of plaster huts which were put up by the South Persia Rifles during the World War — that World War pursues one everywhere — and a Persian Customs House and a Persian Quarantine Officer and a petrol station and an abominable little café, three yards square. That is all. The sun scorches down. And if a breeze does blow for a moment, it simply sweeps the hot sand into one's face.

I shuddered as I tried to imagine what would happen to me if my aeroplane refused to start, if it developed engine-trouble, and I had to spend the night at Jask, in those South Persia huts, without mosquitoe-nets, fans, ice, or anything else.

But my huge Douglas horse was faithful as ever and we sprang up like Perseus on his winged sandals into the air and went on racing to the south.

Incidentally, I got a painful impression of the Persian temperament (or I suppose I should say Iranian temperament) from my all-knowing Captain. After we were well away from Jask, my burly, quiet Netherlander came out of the cockpit and sat down beside me where I was sitting in the forward seat on the left-hand side, which is the best place for seeing the left-hand side of the world as one flies.

"It was a lucky thing," observed my Dutch skipper, "that we had no women aboard when we got to Jask."

"God damn your soul," I shouted, forgetting my manners and the chivalry which is due to one's employes, "God damn your soul! There's no luck about our having no women aboard. It's entirely due to my jolly good sense. Do you suppose," I shouted above the hum of the engines, "that you and I and the Steward, and Sparks, would have had such fun between Amsterdam and Karachi if we'd had women aboard? Don't be a fool."

"As I was saying," replied the Hollander sedately, "it was a lucky thing that we had no women aboard when we got to Jask."

"Oh well!" I said sulkily, "have it your own way. Obviously you want to tell me a story, and you're going to go through with it."

"Bravo!" cried the Steward excitedly, "that's exactly what we said at the capture of Berg-op-Zoom in 1576."

"As I was saying," went on the Captain, unruffled, like all Dutch captains, who are never ruffled by thunder-storms, bad landing-grounds, head winds, or even long official instructions from Headquarters at the Hague.

"As I was saying," said the Captain, "it was a lucky thing we had no women aboard when we got to Jask. It saved us one hour and a quarter."

"Why, Captain?" I enquired.

"No, that isn't strictly true," he went on reflectively, "it might only have cost us forty minutes. If she had been pretty, it would have been an hour and a quarter; if plain, forty minutes."

"So long as I am the charterer of this machine," I said, "she would have been plain. If we have to have women, let's have plain ones. Pretty women are a howling bore."

"Vanity-baggages, as you English say," put in the Steward brightly.

"We don't," I replied, "but we very well might."

"When a woman arrives at Jask," the Captain pursued his course quite unruffled by these verbal air-pockets, "her passport goes, with all the other passports, to the Persian immigration office. It is then taken out of the pile and the photograph is examined by the senior Persian officer. After he has finished, he hands it to the second who examines it and hands it to the third, and so it goes down the scale, through the clerks to the sentries and from the sentries to the chauffeurs, and from the chauffeurs to the sweepers and the scavengers, and from them to any small boys who may be hanging round.

"When a woman comes on to my ship," said the Captain, "and I am on the Far Eastern Route,

I can tell in one minute by her appearance how long my halt in Jask will be, and I arrange my schedule accordingly."

By a queer mischance I had found only that very morning a snapshot of you among my papers. I don't know how it managed to get overlooked when I was tearing up all the rest of them in my flat and making a bonfire of them. It was one of the lot I took at Brighton, the last time we walked along the Sea-wall to Rottingdean — do you remember? — and the wind was blowing from France and you tied that handkerchief round your hair and — oh well, what does it matter? It was that time anyway.

After the Captain had finished his explanation, I fished the photograph out of my pocketbook where I had put it to be safe — by "safe" I mean, of course, in a place where it would catch my eye and so remind me to destroy it — and passed it across to the Captain.

"If you had the misfortune to have a girl like that on board your ship on the Far Eastern Route, how long would you allow for Jask?"

My worthy Hollander looked long and earnestly at the snapshot, and then he handed it back and said gravely and without a flicker, "Nine days. It would seriously upset my schedule," and we all laughed heartily.

I replaced the snap carefully in my pocket-book and tied a knot in my handkerchief. I must tear it up at the first possible opportunity.

Now I'm going to have a look at Karachi. R.

It was a vermilion handkerchief with large white dots on it.

13th April, 1939
Karachi

I got another nasty shock last night. Karachi, it appears, is a sort of aerial Clapham Junction of India, and everyone going on leave and returning from leave — if they can afford to fly — pass through it. I knew that, and so I was more or less resigned to the chances of bumping into some tomfool acquaintance or other in the hotel, and I had my story all ready. I was going to visit the famous rhododendrons in Sikkim and then spend a few weeks in the primula country beyond, and then return by slow stages to England. That was what I was going to say, so I went into the bar with some confidence.

Sure enough the first man I saw was that monumental ass Bobby Watson-Howe, the half-witted cavalryman who used to trail around after you two years ago. You adored his moustache, or his square shoulders, or something. I disliked him quite a lot. However, there he was, his pink cheeks slightly browner and, slightly less chubby, and his manner just as offensive.

"Hullo, Ralph," he said at once — and who the devil ever said he could call me Ralph anyway? — "what are you doing here? Embezzled some cash and skipped out? "

"Certainly not, Watson-Howe," I replied coldly. "I'm going to Sikkim to look at the rhododendrons ——"

"Cissy," he interrupted with an offensive groan.

"And after that," I went on, keeping my temper, "I shall probably go up into the primula country for a few weeks——"

"Pansy," the wretched creature chipped in again.

"And then I shall go home by slow stages."

"I don't believe a word of it," he had the insolence to say. "I bet you're chasing a girl. How's that girl getting on that you were so dotty about? — what was her name? — I made passes at her myself once — you know the one I mean — a pretty little piece with blue eyes — lived somewhere near the BBC — what the devil was her name?"

By this time, as you can imagine, I was getting pretty angry, when luckily — at least I thought it was lucky at the time — a third man joined us, in the uniform of a captain of an Imperial Airways ship, and Watson-Howe introduced us.

"This is the bloke who's taking me home tomorrow," he said, "I shall be seeing the lights of Piccadilly in a minute or two, and then what ho! girls, take care."

The Airways man asked me very civilly if I had been long in Karachi and I, unthinkingly, said no, I'd only been in for about ten minutes. He knitted his brows, sipped his drink, put it down thoughtfully and said, "Come in by train?"

"No, I'm flying," I said, and he knitted his brows again. Then he brightened up all of a sudden and exclaimed, "Oh, then you're the chap who's just landed in the Dutch charter 'plane. I know your Captain. A good lad."

I agreed cordially.

Then to my horror he went on, "I hear you're off to Batavia and that they're coming back alone. My Steward is a pal of your Steward."

"Hullo, hullo, hullo," interposed the loathsome voice of the disgusting cavalryman (couldn't remember your name, blast his leering yellow-dog eyes), "I thought that was a phony yarn you were spinning about Sikkim and rhodo-dam-dendrons. So it's a piece in Batavia you're chasing now, Ralph, is it?"

"I am not chasing a piece in Batavia, damn you," I exclaimed angrily, and that, of course, only made the swine laugh more than ever. The Airways man, being a gentleman, looked down his nose and twiddled his glass.

"Don't tell me it's Bali," cried the facetious cavalryman. "Oh, please don't tell me it's Bali. You haven't joined the noble army of breast-hunters. Oh, Ralph, I believe you have. You naughty old man, you." And much more in the same vein of heavy-handed officers'-mess badinage.

I could have stood all this fourth-form stuff, but his parting shot startled me.

"The first thing I shall do when I get home will be to 'phone the blue-eyed fairy and tell her where her wandering boy is tonight, and how I met him amid snow and ice with a banner with a strange device, KLM."

"You've forgotten her name," I retorted furiously.

"But I've remembered it, my boy, and her address too," and by Jove, he had.

"I'll take her out to supper, old chap, and try a few more passes. Give me the number of your wigwam in Bali and I'll send you a cable and tell you how I get on with the fair wench."

After that I made some excuse and fled, with some more of Watson-Howe's wretched chaff pursuing me through the door.

I had plenty of thinking to do, and it occurred to me that a little fresh air would do me good. So I hired a car and drove slowly into the town past an airship hangar which was built, probably, for the R101, and between wastes of sand-dunes and cactus. I got a nervous jolt — my nervous system having been already considerably jangled by that pestilential horseman — when we came round a corner slap on to the most revolting, sneering, sarcastic camel that I have ever clapped eye upon.

I've seen the ordinary, brown, Zoo camel, and the snuff-coloured Bactrian camel which strides sardonically over the Volga snow-fields in winter and bites impartially anyone who gets within range of his teeth. But this one was black and hairless and really nasty. It appears that the natives shave them and stain them black to keep them cool. It may or may not keep them cool, but it certainly makes them infernally ugly.

After I had got my palpitating nerves a little under control, I went on into the town.

Karachi is a city of broad streets arid space. It rambles in a cheerful old-fashioned way, and its police wear jolly, scarlet turbans, and there is a scent of the sea in the air. I drove down to the sea-front and had a look at the amazing cross between a pier and a promenade which some public-spirited citizen has given to the city, and saw one of the most remarkable private houses which I've ever seen. It was enormous, and was shaped as if it was about five and twenty mosques all rammed together into one enclosure, and it was all bright pink. Pink domes jostled pink minarets behind a pink wall, and pink filigree-work all over the place was just like the icing on the birthday-cake of the youngest daughter of a war profiteer. A large garden-party was obviously just coming to an end, and the road in front of this roseate monstrosity was shining with flowered frocks, Indian splendour, and British top-hats.

In the distance were the derricks and smoke and funnels of the harbour, and beyond them again the hills of Baluchistan. I got out of my car and leant for a while on the balustrade of the pier, and wondered about Watson-Howe, and you, and my chances of getting to the Islands of Javan and Gadire, and attaining to Freedom at last.

Kim's old lama knew a thing or two. He wanted to get free of the Wheel of Life, and I suppose he got nearer to freedom from the Wheel than most human beings in fact or fiction. I'll never get anywhere near the sort of freedom that the lama was aiming at, and I don't think I want it, but I'm most emphatically going to get the sort I *am* aiming at, even if I have to hide in the hills of Baluchistan to get it. But I hope it won't come to that. I'll get to those islands yet.

On that pier I thought out a new scheme for circumventing you and your spies — Good Lord! I wonder if you planted that infernal soldier in the bar of the Karachi hotel, and if you've planted them all over India. The Indian Army was always one of your best recruiting areas, wasn't it? Do you remember that major with the glossy moustache who was so silly that he made Watson-Howe seem to be only just sub-human? And the brigadier who could read and write as well? I wonder if they're all posted at bars at this very moment in every garrison town in India. It's a disquieting thought. However, I must take a chance. I've got to cross India somehow.

So this is what I worked out. The Far Eastern Route is a little too dangerous, so I'm going to skip off it for a time.

By the time you get this, it will be too late for you to do anything, and I will have dodged across. And just to keep your spies actively engaged with what they imagine to be their brains, I am sending my 'plane on without me, with orders to wait for me at a certain rendezvous a very long way from here.

With a much more cheerful heart I drove back to the airport and sneered openly at every camel I met. Indeed I sneered so well that most of them started back in alarm, and looked quite human for a moment.

Watson-Howe was no longer visible. Doubtless he was despatching you a long telegram. He'll be ringing you up in three days. Give him a kiss from me and have a nice time with him. R.

P.S. — He couldn't remember your name — blast his soul — the only name that ever was of any real importance in the world. But perhaps he was right. In a month even I will have forgotten it.

P.P.S. — "There is no name with whatever emphasis of passionate love repeated, of which the echo is not faint at last." Watson-Howe and Landor both hit upon the same truth, though perhaps they expressed it in different words.

Same Day
In the Air — Secret

I'm away off on my big dodge across India. It is just like the Knight's move at chess. And the Knight's move is the only move on the board which really baffles the Queen, with all her arrogant and offensive and confident dashings hither and thither. She sweeps here and she sweeps there and she thinks herself most remarkably clever, but the cunning little Knight sidesteps, and the Queen has to scratch her golden head and think again.

This is what I have done. I sent my Netherlanders eastwards while I chartered another 'plane — a 'plane belonging to an Indian company and manned by a small Parsee Pilot and a small Parsee Wireless Operator — and flew off gaily down the coast of India to Bombay. When I say gaily, I don't mean that I was gay all the time. Far from it. Very far from it indeed.

At first, frankly, I was petrified with fear. After the magnificent expanse of the wings on my great Douglas, this contraption seemed about the size of a match-box. And it gave the impression that it was made of the same material as a matchbox. It quivered and it danced, and it flirted up and down even in a perfectly quiet atmosphere. And when it met an air-pocket it became just a cork in the pool at the foot of a waterfall. It bounced. That is the only word I can think of to describe the sensation. And we were lucky if we only bounced up and down. Sometimes we rolled from side to side as well.

And to add the touch which almost pushed me into a state of hysterics, every time we bounced, the little Pilot turned to the little Sparks and whistled gravely, and the little Sparks whistled gravely back. It turned out afterwards that that was their method of telling each other that they were having a nice day and enjoying the trip.

But I didn't know that at the time, and it's at the time that one wants to know these things. Afterwards isn't half so helpful.

But there was one thing which the Douglas and the Indian 'planes had in common, and which both crews had in common, and that was complete efficiency. The midget Pilot made beautiful landings everywhere, and I imagine the midget Sparks understood what he was doing with his knobs and keys, because everything worked out exactly.

Still, the first hour or two of the flight really was frightening, after my Dutchmen, and there was no freedom-loving Steward on board with his every-ready glass of Dutch beer. And the situation was not helped by the scene below.

Hardly were we clear of Karachi than we were flying over a really weird country. So far, on this flight from a demoiselle, I have seen some pretty quaint sights, and some tolerably beautiful ones. I mean the Gulf of Corinth, and Mussolini's George Robeys, and the Parthenon, and the Jordan Valley, and the Persian coast and the Basra Ganymede — to speak of only a few — are a fair medley. They range from the grim to the comic, with some little touches of beauty thrown in here and there.

But none of them were weird as the Great Rann of Kutch is weird.

The Great Rann (pronounced Run, as in cricket) is an enormous desert, and here it occurs to me that you are getting a devilish fine correspondence-course in general knowledge, my small angel. If you are reading these letters you will be acquiring information at a great rate, which will help you a lot when you dine out with elderly and amorous peers and dashing, bald financiers, and fat fools.

For example, the conversation at Quag's might go like this:

Elderly and Amorous Peer: Will you come up tonight to see my collection of silhouettes?

Small Angel: The Great Run of Kutch is an enormous desert.

E. and A.P.: May I show you my unique collection of hussar-fronted pyjamas?

Small Angel: I am told on the best possible authority that the waterways in Basra are fringed with oleander.

E. and A.P.: I live in Park Lane.

Small Angel: Athena the Maid had a temple called the Parthenon.

E. and A.P.: Oh! hell.

You see the idea. Are you becoming Mayfair's Mine of Information? Are you degenerating from the position of Queen of the World to just little Mrs. Know-all?

It would be a picturesque revenge — not that I want to avenge anything or that I feel even faintly revengeful. I am too distantly remote for any rot of that sort. Flight, in an aeroplane, is so swift that the past drops behind like an exhausted blue-bottle. It was. And so it isn't. I am so remote from the past, even the past of a week ago, that it no longer is in my mind. What do you look like? I've forgotten. On which side was the twist of your little mouth? What was the slant of your Correggio-head when you were teasing? What the magnolia colour of your neck? What the slenderness of your fingers? I've forgotten. I've forgotten everything.

So blessed a thing is Flight.

An American makes a machine. A Dutchman buys it. I hire it. And a whole life is re-made. And a silly little girl fades into the poppy-dust of oblivion.

Your name was repeated — heavens! how often — with an emphasis of passionate love. But never no more. Mr. Douglas and Messrs. KLM (which stands, though you mightn't think it, for Koninklijke Luchtvaart Maatschappij) have seen to that, and the echo is faint at last (after five days).

So blessed, and so swift, a thing is Flight.

I was talking about the Great Rann of Kutch and how it added materially to my tremors when the lads were whistling to each other in the bumps.

The Rann is an endless desert of pure white salt. It seems that once it was part of the Indian Ocean and that an earthquake shut it off from the Ocean so that it became an inland salt lake. The sun soon dried off the water, leaving only the salt. So as far as the eye can reach (from a bouncing but efficient match-box) the land is the purest white.

Strangest thing of all, a river comes over the north-eastern horizon — a big blue river, lovely against the salt — and meanders down through the whiteness and disappears vaguely in the middle of it all. It just evaporates. At first you can't believe your eyes. At first you think you must be above the clouds and that this curving blue ribbon must be just a freakish rift in the clouds which lets you see the Indian Ocean. Then you realize that the whiteness isn't the whiteness of clouds, and you ask the Parsee Wireless Operator, and he whistles ominously and you shrink back, frightened, in your seat.

The whiteness goes on and on and on, and you toy with the idea of asking the pilot what makes it so white (because, of course, you don't find out about the earthquake and the salt business until you reach Bombay and are talking to a High Court judge at a swagger dinner-party), but you don't ask him because you know he would only whistle ominously too, and then the 'plane goes up three storeys in a split second and turns over to do the crawl stroke for a split second which seems like a quarter of an hour, and then it drops to the mezzanine, and you begin to think, Oh, to the devil with the Great Rann of Kutch, and I wish I was back in Holland.

Which is very unjust. Because the Rann gave me the weirdest sight of my life.

My little pilot made his first landing at Bhuj, the capital — so they tell me — of the State of Kutch. I spoke to a man in Bombay about the place, and he said, off-handedly, "Oh yes, Bhuj. A little place. I know it well. Some pagodas, and a mosque or two, and a traffic in dates."

That man was an ass.

Bhuj is an ancient walled city, just as walled as Avila or Rothenburg or Visby in Gottland. It is a mediaeval town. And, what's more, outside Bhuj there is a solitary, rocky, oblong hill which has a wall, with towers and out-flanking bastions and barbicans, running the whole way round the high places of the hill, rather like Carcassonne.

So far as I could see, no one lives inside that wall on the rock. It seemed to be a derelict monument built by fighting men of the past. But even so, I thought the wall was as worth while a mention as a nice chaffering of dates.

After we left Bhuj my spirits went up a lot, in spite of a total absence of beer at the airport.

There were three reasons for encouragement. Firstly, I had seen an Indian mediaeval fortress; secondly, my little Pilot had made a faultless landing; and thirdly, he had made a faultless start.

To make my life even more pleasant, the head wind that we had been battering our noses against abated, and we skimmed gracefully down, like a may-fly, on to the Juhu aerodrome of Bombay.

So here I am in Bombay, Little One.

And I'm not going near any hotel bars. Your spies may be all over the place, but they won't learn anything. I know such swagger people here that I won't be consorting with the riffraff who claim to adore you, in their Staff-College way, in their Le Touquet-Deauville way, in their what-a-jolly-little-girl-you-are way.

No, Miss. In Bombay, I'm out of your class.

I'm sorry. But it just can't be helped. You were a sweet girl, but not quite on my Bombay level.

I can't write any more. I must rush off to dress to dine with the Governor.

No, I'll be fair. You don't spend all your life in restaurants with fools. I wish you did. It would make it so much easier to forget you quickly. The sort of thing that makes it hard is the remembrance of that time you played darts with that small eight-year-old girl and looked at her so sweetly and lovingly, and taught her funny little games, and acted funny little pieces for her. Nobody can be wholly bad who was adored by a babe as you were adored by that babe. Nobody can be written off as adamantine and cruel who was so gentle. R.

14th April, 1939
Bombay

Well, my vaguely-remembered snippet, here I am in the heart of the British Raj. And I must say that the British Raj is very, very like the British Raj. By that I mean that the real thing is what one expected it to be like. The East is exactly like the East.

All the photographs of myself in days long since, in the arms of an ayah, are just like children in the arms of an ayah. All the Kipling descriptions of the natives going up and down the dusty roads are just like the natives going up and down the dusty roads. The palm-trees, the crowds, the heat, the colours, the Maidan, the flocks of men in the evening, all dressed in white, the tapering lights of Back Bay as they go out into the sea, the mysterious little houses with glimpses of hideous interiors, the people sleeping on the pavement under the dim lamps, the lovely old building of the Town Hall with its Greek columns, — all that I was ready for. All that was in Kipling, in the photographs of my very early youth, and in the conversation, inescapable, of certain senior officers in certain clubs.

But not even Rudyard or photographs or bores had got me ready for some things.

No one had told me how beautiful Bombay is. No one in England had advised me to stand in the gardens on Malabar Hill, where the Ladies' Gymkhana used to be, and look across Back Bay and down across the roofs of the City. There are new massive blocks of flats on the far side, and the oldest inhabitants grumble about them. I thought they added to the beauty of the view, just as Chicago's skyscrapers make Michigan Boulevard one of the great streets of the world.

Back Bay isn't blue, in the sense that the Aegean is blue, or the Mediterranean, or your eyes. It is more of a pearly grey — at least it is as I see it today — so that the mist and the Bay get together on the horizon.

Another thing that no one had told me to look out for: the view from the Yacht Club lawn across the harbour to the faint shadow of the hills at Matheran. I think it is as beautiful as the Malabar view of Back Bay. I'm not sure that it isn't more beautiful.

Back Bay is static. There is nothing except loveliness, and a couple of fisher-boats, and a floating corpse or two, and a mass of sightseers, pedlars, and flaming orators on the narrow beach.

On the other side, the harbour-side, there is loveliness too, but it is dynamic. At any moment a gun may fire and a fleet of little sailing-boats may flock out and jockey against each other in the sunlight. A white liner may nose its penin-sular and oriental way to the dock-side. A cruiser may wander past.

And toward sun-down an eager figure will stand on every vessel within sight, waiting for the signal to haul down the flag from the mast-head. When the flag comes down from the official mast on shore, the eager figures leap to their lanyards (or main braces, or sheets, or something) and haul like mad, so that a hundred flags come fluttering down and chaps like me sit on the lawn of the Yacht Club and lazily drink a gin-and-lime and reflect that it is a privilege to belong to a stern island race. Sons of the sea, that is what we are, and it puts a glow into the old sea-dog's heart — as he quaffs his gimlet — to see the synchronization of that flag-hauling.

But that is what I mean when I say that the harbour-side of Bombay is dynamic, whereas Back Bay is static. The one is like a woman who is so beautiful that she relies on her face to do her business for her. The other is like a woman who also is beautiful, but who is clever enough to know that vivacity will defeat the dumb blonde every time. As a matter of fact, now that I come to think of it, the same thing applies exactly to you. You are beautiful enough — the Lord who made you knows — to rest on your spurious laurels and be a sort of feminine Back Bay. If you had done that, you would have wrecked quite enough lives and gone down to a sort of static posterity. If you had done that, there wouldn't really be any legitimate complaint against you.

But to add a lightning wit to your beauty; to kindle a sparkle in blue eyes; to fire guns and sail exciting yacht races; to convert Back Bay into Bombay Harbour; — no, no, no, that wasn't fair; that wasn't right.

To look divine is one thing. There are ten thousand shop-girls, and several in the middleclasses, who look divine. But to be divine as well, oh, no! Not fair. Not cricket. Definitely not cricket.

And that's a neat idea too. I shall never see you again, and I shall never see Lord's again. So what does it matter to me whether your beauty and your wit and your understanding are cricket or not? In the islands of Rarotonga, or wherever it is that I shall fetch up, we may occasionally bowl down a cocoanut to each other — on a cocoanut-matting pitch, of course — but we won't bother our heads about you.

The sound of surf upon beaches, and the click of nuts on bats, will be all the music that we shall want — with some small assistance from the short-wave broadcasts from that cranky place just in front of your house. We won't want the echo of your voice. Nor will we want the image

of your face. Nor the subtlety of your understanding: Nor the aurora borealis of your wit.

So clear out. If you don't mind, just clear out. And stay out.

If I haven't made myself clear, what I am trying to say is, Clear out and stay out.

Let's go back.

The other thing which nobody told me about in Bombay is the mango. Naturally I had heard about the mango ever since my ayah dandled me in her arms, in a London suburb. I suppose I must have been told, anything from two to three hundred times in my life, by warriors of the North West Frontier and survivors of the Black Hole, that I hadn't lived till I'd tasted a Bombay mango. I never protested, from two to three hundred times, that I hadn't ever tasted a mango and that I was living very nicely, thank you; because I'm a tolerant soul who hates vexing majors and colonels.

But, you know, those absurd field-officers were right. The mango is delicious. And you're encouraged by the local Mem-sahibs to gobble it without regard for your ears. They don't mind, these broadminded Mems, if the stray guest finds that towards the end of desert, he has to disentangle bits of mangoes from his lobes.

In effect, mangoes are the goods.

My host here in Bombay says that they are bad for the liver. What I say is, give me mangoes and I'll take a chance on cirrhosis.

It is very hot. It is hotter than any place I've ever been in. But there is always a breeze from the sea which saves my life.

Two Hours later

A rather odd situation has arisen. My host took me aside just now and asked if I would like to drive tomorrow up to the Ghats. (The Ghats seem to be hills or something, eighty miles away.) I said, respectfully and deferentially, as from a guest to a host, no, I would sooner not drive up into the Ghats. He said, fine, we'll all drive up into the Ghats to-morrow. He said, we'll start at half-past six in the morning. That'll suit you? he said.

"I don't want to be a spoil-sport," I said.

"That's all right," he interrupted, "you don't have to be."

"But," I went on, still diffidently, "I'm not feeling very well. In fact, I haven't got accustomed to Eastern cooking yet, and I'm rather upset inside my tummy. So if you don't mind, I'd sooner not go for a long motor-drive tomorrow."

My host was all concern at once.

"Not feeling well in your tummy?" he cried. "That's just too bad. Well, well, well, that's just too bad." He pondered a moment, and then brightened up. "Never mind," he said, "you'll be all right in the morning. We'll start at half-past six. Don't be late."

And with that he went to bed.

So I must stop scribbling to you if I've got to get up at five-thirty in the morning and drive, in a weak state of digestion, to an unknown destination eighty miles away.

I feel rather benevolent towards you this evening, rather like an uncle who has paid a visit to a nephew at a prep-school and has given him a mass of butterscotch in the sincere hope that he will never see the little beast again. R.

With me it isn't a sincere hope: it's a certainty.

15th April, 1939
Bombay

If ever a man was convinced, by one single episode, of the existence of an All-Seeing Eye, that man is me.

A thing happened today which would convert the most bigoted Agnostic, a thing so timed, so just, so witty, and so utterly in harmony with the Ultimate God, that it would be unthinkable to dismiss it as the product of irresponsible Chance. Listen and you shall judge for yourself.

I spent a miserable night — if the brief stretch of hours between midnight and 5.30 A.M. can be called a night — tossing about in the heat and suffering from acute indigestion. At 5.30 A.M., that ungodly hour, I was harried out of bed by a bevy of silent Indians and I managed to be ready at 6.35, only five minutes late.

"Hm!" remarked my host, "thought you had cried off after all," and with that we piled into the car.

My host drove and his wife sat beside him, and I sat behind with the daughter of the house and various packages and picnic rugs and all the usual odds and ends which accumulate in a family car. As the host's legs are very long, quite as long as mine, he had pushed the driving-seat as far back as possible, so that I sat with my knees under my chin, a position which a man suffering from indigestion does not normally choose of his own free will.

So we started off and in ten minutes we were back again because I had forgotten my topee. The host put on an artificial expression of resignation, and he looked at his watch, and he wondered to himself, but quite loud enough for me to hear, if it was worth while making the expedition at all now that we'd lost so much time.

However, we got started again, and off we went, on the Poona military road, which is one of the only two roads out of Bombay, and so embarked upon the most ghastly journey I have ever done — and that includes bumping over Kutch, trains through Russia in winter not long after the Revolution, walking sixteen miles through a snow-blizzard in Poland with the wind against me, riding up to the Somme battle past the corner of Mametz Wood in a 5.9 howitzer barrage, running away from a pursuing pack of Huns at Cambrai, being motored from

San Francisco to Los Angeles at an average speed of sixty-three mph for eight consecutive hours, and sitting between Oxford Circus and Hatchard's bookshop in Piccadilly in a very small car that was nominally being guided by your lily-white hands and controlled by your jack-o'-lanthorn brain.

All those are journeys which have left a searing mark upon my soul.

But Bombay to Khandala on the old Poona Road beat the lot.

At first we bowled along a moderately good road in the cool of the morning. I mean it wasn't much hotter than a July noon-tide in Surrey, and the road wasn't much worse than a side road in Aberdeenshire that has been due for repairs for some little while.

After an hour or so we reached a less good road, and the sun mounted the heavens, and after another half-hour we halted for breakfast under a tree on the edge of a cactus-dotted expanse of sand.

I wasn't feeling in my best form, and the ravens secured most of my breakfast, and a pair of kites which flapped heavily round overhead seemed to regard me as a potential corpse already. A coppersmith-bird sat in the branches and hammered away at his nerve-racking monotone, and some dun-coloured cows came mooching up to see what the ravens were making such a fuss about, and a crowd of small children mysteriously appeared out of the uninhabited stretch of cactus. Then we pushed on. The road grew worse and worse. Often road-repairs were in progress — and not one second too soon — and we had to make detours across fields where the deep ruts were full of light dust. But it was impossible to say that the fields were really any worse than the unrepaired road.

The sun gained steadily in brassy efficiency and a nice sultry wind blew the dust about in capital style. Also, as it was a public holiday, every vehicle that could make the grade was in action, for it seems that the Indians are inveterate travellers. If they are somewhere they instinctively crave to be elsewhere, and the old Poona Road was whizzing with motor-buses, packed up to the roof, and kicking up any dust that the burning sirocco hadn't managed to hoist into the air.

The car was one of those big American saloons and my host, who is a superb driver, has a theory that it is more comfortable to traverse a bad road quickly than slowly. So it may be, if you are sitting in the front seat, nicely slung between the two axles. But it's not such a good theory for the chaps behind.

Also, by some trick of aerodynamics, when you are travelling quickly, the dust only enters in solid masses by the back windows. Of course, the people who are sitting at the back can always get over the difficulty by shutting all their windows. It is true that thereby they will suffocate, but maybe they prefer suffocation through lack of air to being stifled by dust. Anyway, it's for them to choose, and anyway the inheritors of the Raj ought to be made of sterner stuff and not worry about such trifles.

Actually the daughter of the house and I tried both ways, and finally decided on being stifled by the dust, literally pulverized.

So we pounded on, leaping from rut to rut, and the hot wind poured in, and the Indian sun rose to its full height, and I longed for an iced whisky-and-soda, and Death, and a cold bath, and my Dutchmen, and the clean soft snow of Russia, and a shot of morphine, and above all I longed to be anywhere in the world (your presence always excepted) rather than on the Poona Road between Bombay and Khandala.

I can't tell you how many thatched villages we passed through, and how many million brown babies sprawled at the roadside, and what droves of buffaloes looked sourly at us. Buffaloes, they tell me, dislike white men so intensely that they attack them on sight. It's an odd feeling to find oneself sympathising with buffaloes, because they are not easy creatures to look at.

I had begun to despair of ever seeing Sourabaya, and the Seven Isles where Freya lived, and the Rajah Laut's country, by the time we reached the foothills of the Ghats. My throat was so dusty that I couldn't speak, even if the state of my tummy hadn't been so discouraging to light conversation, and my knees were getting bruised from the incessant bangings against my chin, and I need hardly say that I had cramp, in both legs.

It wasn't as if the Ghats were any cooler. We had to climb and climb in first gear, and the engine got almost red-hot, and the sun beat down.

At last, after about four hours that might have been forty for all I knew, we reached the top and halted to look back at the view. As I couldn't see out of my blood-shot eyes, I didn't even pretend to look, so I haven't the faintest idea what the view was like, but from the spry and eager applause of the host and hostess, both as fresh as daisies, it was possible to gather that the view was a regular pippin as views go.

"Cheer up," cried the host genially, giving me a most almighty smack on the back so that a cloud of dust rose into the air out of my clothes, cars, eyes, nostrils, hair, neck, shoes, and fingernails, "Cheer up. We're only a hundred yards from the hotel, and in three minutes we'll be sitting down to the longest stoup of iced lager-beer that has been seen by mortal man."

At that precise instant the All-Seeing Eye interposed, and my host saw that his off-side back tyre was flat.

"Whether or not you'll be sitting down to iced lager-beer in three minutes," I managed to croak through my cracking lips, "is entirely for you to decide. I certainly will be." And with that I stumped off down the road. And by God, I was.

I doubt if ever a more ecstatic sensation has ever come the way of a human being. In one moment Injustice had been defeated; in one moment an honest man's Thirst had been put well on the way to satisfaction; in one moment an Agnostic's faith had been restored.

As I lugged my poor, cramp-beset legs down that last hundred yards of dusty furnace, I sang in my heart a huge Te Deum. Half-an-hour earlier I would have laid my head under a cactus and sung a Nunc Dimittis — with an extra prayer that it should be a very prompt Dimittis.

But on those last hundred yards, my song was a Glorification. I reached, tottering but inspired, the hotel on the edge of the jungle, and in a jiffy I was slaking the immemorial thirst of the East with the lager of Denmark, produced straight out of a refrigerator from America.

And, after I had drunk three of these long Danish lagers, I lay back in my chair and contemplated the imminent jungle, and hoped that my host was enjoying himself with his busted tyre. It was at this moment, after three lagers, and after a quiet contemplation of the jungle, with a picture in my mind of that wheel being changed under the burning sun and in the middle of the sirocco-driven dust, that I thought, suddenly, that there must be a God.

The whole essence of Life is timing. You can fall madly in love with a girl in March and she pays no attention to you, because she is busy trailing after a pasty-faced gigolo with a light tenor voice. In April the suet-gigolo has gone to Biarritz, taking his alto trills with him, to raise some dibs off an Argentinian widow who is rich and dismal, but passionate. So in May the girl comes back to you, tripping hither, tripping thither, in a sort of modern minuet, arranged for love-making. But by that time, the beginning of June, you are off in pursuit of a dark girl from the provinces who is almost at once elected Carpet Queen of Axminster and goes to Hollywood in a bathing-suit on the strength of it, and is never heard of again. And you are left in the end exactly where you started — a flop. Unless you get your timing right, you might just as well chuck your hand in.

This brings me back to my three iced lagers and my unexpected belief in God. If ever there was a stupendous bit of timing, it was that puncture.

And so now I am a believer in the All-Seeing Eye.

The rest of the day was by comparison humdrum.

Within half-an-hour the amateur mechanic arrived with his large automobile. The wheel had been changed under the Sun of India. He was very hot, and very dusty, and very thirsty, and ominously silent. After a bit I got the impression that I ought to have stayed and helped him with the wheel-changing — held the bolts, and handed the nuts, and sweated at the jack, and given useful advice, and so on.

But I didn't. I blissfully concentrated upon Denmark's lager, and heartily congratulated him upon his success as a wheel-changer. My congratulations somehow didn't go with a big swing.

We bathed in a pool in the jungle. We drank gimlets. We had lunch on a terrace and watched the chameleons playing on the tree-trunks. We listened to the little noises of the jungle. We had a siesta. And then we drove back, very fast, on the corrugated tracks which are called the Poona Road, through the dust-storms, past the buffaloes.

The hot wind was hotter than ever and the dust was thicker and the back axle was more unyielding. There were more people than ever in the villages, and the space between the driving-seat and my seat visibly shrank. Cramp, sand-blindness, suffocation, thirst, and general malaise competed with each other for the high-spot of discomfort, and all galloped home triumphantly in a quintuple dead-heat.

We got back at last, and I had a cold bath and a very strong drink, and managed to convey to my host's butler, whispering, and speaking very slowly, that there was nothing in the world I wanted so much, that there was nothing else in the world that I would pay as high a fee as one rupee eight annas for, as a quiet five minutes with a railway timetable which would tell me how to get out of Bombay.

The timetable arrived and an escape was plotted. But the escape didn't materialize. My host, after the bitterness of death was past, as Agag said in the Old Testament, abandoned the jungle for civilization, and I basked in the famous clubs of Bombay — the Willingdon, with its subtle little golf-course; the Yacht Club, looking over towards Matheran and within an inch of the large archway which is called the Gateway to India, and which of course it isn't (the Gateway to India is the Suez Canal; or, even more truly, Scapa Flow, where the Fleet lies watching); and by far the most exciting, the Byculla Club.

I don't think I've ever spent a more romantic evening — outside your company in the old days, you poor little fish — than I have just spent on the lawns of the Byculla Club.

The whole of British India is on these lawns. How many generations of merchants, and civil servants, and doctors, and soldiers, and administrators, and adventurers, have sat out here in the starlight and talked and planned and lived, while the everlasting murmur of the native quarters, on all four sides, rustles and hums beyond the limits of the club's compound? How many generations of men, father and son, father to son, have lived in these white-washed buildings in their life's work of serving India?

There is much that can be said against the Raj, but there is a hell of a lot more to be said in favour of the Raj. And when I went through the high, cool rooms and saw the — how shall I say? — the sort of dignified permanence and stability of it all, I was moved to think of that old stuff in Ecclesiasticus about praising famous men and our fathers who begat us.

Whatever may be the future of India and the British Raj, nothing can take away from the Byculla Club its position as the essential heart of Britain in India. There may be other places which are apparently far more important. But this space of green grass and trees and lovely old buildings and traditions is really the essence of it all — a quiet place of order and common-sense and reason and discipline among the discordant noises of the Orient.

But time presses. I must make my Knight's move quickly or the Queen may pounce.

The railway-guide is on my dressing-table, and I must on. I must on. I hate to leave this beautiful city of Bombay. A few minutes ago I wandered into the gardens where the Ladies' Gymkhana used to be, and looked along to Malabar Point and the long thin strip of land opposite, which ends at Colaba, and I thought I had seen few sights more lovely. But it is no good hanging around simply because Malabar Point is beautiful, and because at any moment I may see the Governor's escort of brightly-coloured horsemen come clattering past.

There is sterner work afoot. There is a Flight from a Lady to be accomplished.

So tonight I leave the air and sneak across India in an air-conditioned train.

If I could spare a pennyweight of love from the love I feel for Bombay I would send it to you, but I can't, so I don't, and I doubt if I would anyway. R.

Girls are kept in their place here.

16th April, 1939
Air-Conditioned Train

This is a crafty device of mine, small one. What a hope have you got of extracting me from Asia now? I'm hiding in a trans-Indian train, and your battery of silk-moustachioed spies are completely baffled. While they are haunting — and aren't they a set of ghosts? — the Juhu airport, I'm jogging laboriously towards Calcutta in what I call an air-conditioned train and what your cavalry pals would probably describe as a "ruddy puff puff, eh?"

It's very ingenious, and I'm pleased with the idea. While you hunt 'planes, I obscurely, almost dingily, travel by train.

It is going to take me thirty-six hours, and I shall cross the heart of India, so I had better literally glue my eye — as they say — to the window of my carriage.

But as Bombay's hospitality has had a sleep-inducing effect on me, I think I will snatch forty winks and go on later.

Later

I have just woken up with a jerk exactly opposite the white-washed buildings and the smart, tidy gardens of a Borstal Institute! Can one never escape from prisons and institutes and reformatories and restraints? At every step comes a reminder that some poor devil is on a chaingang somewhere. Probably the wretched children in this white-washed Institute at Narighpor, or whatever it is called, are compelled to do the white-washing and the gardening, and are then taught to be proud of the jobs which they've been forced to do. It's the same with every chain-gang. In a bad temper I tried to go to sleep again, but couldn't. The noise of the train-wheels was full of a clanking which sounded like fetters. So I'll sit up and scribble to you, who are tearing your curls at this moment, I know, and crying bitterly at the sight of the empty kennel and the smashed chain and the fetters that have been so skilfully filed through.

It is a very strange thing how the word "Escape" is a word that is respectfully admired all the world over, whereas the word "Escapist" is sneered at.

Think of some of the famous Escapes. Odysseus sending his men out of the cave of the Cyclops by tying them underneath a lot of sheep (big, strong sheep, or else very little fellows); Cervantes escaping from the Moors; Casanova creeping out of the Leads at Venice; Prince Charles Edward on his journey across the Western Highlands; the boat-party which left the Emden to destroy the wireless-station at the Cocos Islands in the Pacific and, having watched instead the destruction of the Emden, escaped in an open boat and reached Berlin. Think of Lord Nithsdale whose wife extracted him from the Tower against all the guards of the German Kings of England. Think of the Escaping Club of the World War, of which the king-pin was Major Johnny Evans, who played cricket for England against Australia, and who was the only man in the War who escaped twice — once from the Boche and once from Gentleman Johnny Turk. Those men, Buckley and Medlicott and Evans, and all the rest of them, weren't they heroes?

And aren't they admired as heroes, with the Irish patriots who got out of Lincoln jail, and the man who painted his face to look like a waterlily and floated on his back down the German moat between the sentries?

But Escapism is regarded as something cowardly. How damned silly most people are when they start using words they don't understand. As if I am doing something cowardly in escaping from you! I am, morally, in the class of Evans and Casanova — no, no, I don't mean what you mean. I am referring to my moral resemblance to Casanova in his capacity as escaper.

We are brave men, we, and we take our lives in our hands when we creep out in aeroplanes, or over roofs, or across moats.

It was thoughts of this kind that made me angry as we chugged along through the sands of India from the Borstal boys.

But my natural sunny disposition was quite restored by the sight of a bird that was blue as any kingfisher.

There's something wonderful about a bird that really is bright blue. The green woodpecker of the Surrey Commons, with its gay head and its flight that goes up and down like a scenic railway, is attractive enough, but it can never touch the halcyon. Incidentally, I don't agree for one moment with the scholars who say that the derivation of "halcyon-days" is that, the kingfisher makes its nest in the Aegean Sea in the first fourteen days of December, when the sea is said to be very calm. I am quite sure that "halcyon-days" are days on which you see a kingfisher. I saw one on the Itchen many years ago, and I saw another on the little river which runs below the great Castle of Bouillon near the Ardennes. But those are my only two halcyon-days.

The bird I have just seen from my train was nearly as good, but it just hadn't quite got the finishing sparkle. Maeterlinck had one good idea in his life when he wrote a play called "The Blue Bird."

So far there have been a surprising number of trees, but now we are getting nearer to Central India and the trees and the stubble-fields are gradually fading into a desert of stones and scrubby little bushes which are very like the great desert of Arizona. There's plenty of cactus too, just like Arizona, only here it flowers with a bright yellow flower, whereas there, so far as I can remember, the flower was reddish, — though as a matter of fact it may not have been flowering at all in Arizona, because I passed through that desert with one of the finest hangovers that has ever come out of Los Angeles, and that is something, and so I'm not a qualified judge.

Although the landscape is incredibly dreary, there are bright patches — birds and cactus flowers, and always some colours round the village-well where the women are drawing water. And, of course, the stations are a mass of coloured humanity. The more I see of Central India the more certain I am that there are only two occupations. One is toiling under a blazing sun in fields which look as if they could not raise a couple of cabbages, and the other is sitting in railway stations waiting for a train.

But there isn't really any point in my trying to describe this journey. You will find it all written down very much better in the chapter in Kim about the perpetual movement on the Grand Trunk Road. There you will find all the colours and the restlessness and the futile and trivial bustlings of these people.

"All castes and kinds of men move here. Look! Brahmins and chumars, bankers and tinkers, barbers and bunnias, pilgrims and potters — all the world going and coming. It is to me as a river from which I am withdrawn like a log after a flood."

In fact, God's India is exactly like Kipling's India, and I who was brought up in an AngloIndian household with pictures and photographs all round me and the works of Kipling in the nursery bookcase, find nothing new or strange in all these sights. I am only seeing what I expected to see, or rather what I have seen in my mind's eye ever since I can remember.

On the platform at Jubbulpore there were the traditional English officers, neat, dapper Lords of the World, quietly waiting until somebody came to tell them that their carriage was ready for them. And, in the sunshine beyond, the kites were strolling round the sky exactly as I had always known that Chil, the Kite, strolled round in the sky of the Mowgli stories.

This journey is like living in a dream of the past. Nothing is new. It is all precisely what I have known subconsciously for so many years.

I doubt if a citizen of any other race will ever understand the mysterious link between Britain and India. Somewhere else Kipling says that there are certain names which crop up throughout the story of the Raj. "Some people will tell you that if there were but a single loaf of bread in all India it would be divided equally between the Plowdens, the Trevors, the Beadons, and the Rivett-Carnacs. That is only one way of saying that certain families serve India generation after generation as dolphins follow in line across the open sea."

These are families who have served India for many generations, but the link is also strong in families that have only been out for two generations. I suppose the reason is that England and Scotland are littered with retired Anglo-Indians who keep the tradition alive at dinner-tables and garden-parties.

Jack Squire wrote about these people in a poem called "Winter Nightfall," about the old, yellow, stucco house that was empty and decaying, and someone told him that the old retired Colonel — "Some Fraser or Murray" — was the last person to live in it.

> Did he turn through his doorway
> And go to his study,
> And light many candles?
> And fold in the shutters,
> And heap up the fireplace
> To fight off the damps?
> And muse on his boyhood,
> And wonder if India
> Ever was real?
> And shut out the loneliness
> With pig-sticking memoirs
> And collections of stamps?

But whatever the reason, there is this queer link, and it will take more than Mr. Gandhi and all his Congress friends to break it.

So if you want to know about Central India, have a look at *Kim* and don't bother me with questions about goats and cows and people working in the sun. Take it from me it is all exactly like India. R.

P.S. — I was wrong about the halcyon-days. You gave me one or two in your time. And I am grateful to you for them.

18th April, 1939
In my Douglas Again

There obviously was no such thing as the Black Hole of Calcutta. Calcutta itself is the Black Hole. I got there in the middle of a heat-wave in the middle of their hot weather. The town is made of dirty ginger-bread, and it looks as if it would tumble over at any minute. There are thousands of people in the streets, and hundreds of sacred cows on the pavement, and the heat, and the heat, and the heat.

So, utterly exhausted, I hired a cab at the station and drove to Dum-Dum, the airport, and there I found my brave Dutchmen waiting for me.

The Douglas was lying outside the hangar with its engines turning over quietly; Sparks was calling Amsterdam to get weather reports from Burma; the Steward was oiling his corkscrew; the Second Pilot was arranging the clearance-papers; the Mechanic was oiling his engines; and the Captain was quietly waiting orders. We all fell on each other's necks, clambered into the ship, and started off once again. Little matchboxes and air-conditioned trains are all very well in their way, but give me the wide span of the silver Douglas.

Before we made the sprint across the Bay of Bengal we turned westwards for a few minutes to look at the Ganges — a long, white, thin thread twisting into the distance across the brown plains, visible for miles and miles and miles. I suppose I ought to go and glance at Benares, but I can't be bothered. So, after a look at the Holy River, we turn again and go eastwards over the Delta of the Ganges as it trickles into the Bay in a thousand arms, here through sand and there through dense forests.

We now strike out over the Bay of Bengal and there is nothing to see.

I may add to this letter in a few hours.

. . . . .

Later

Here we are over the flat coast of Burma. There are little islands and inland waterways, sometimes three or four or five of them running parallel with each other and parallel with the coast. It is all thickly wooded, and I can see three big fires where the natives are making clearings for next year's crops. The whole land is a mixture of grey earth and brown rock and forest. We turn inland over mountains which are scarred with the diggings of tin-prospectors — just as Montana is scarred with the gold-hunters and Nevada with the silver-hunters — and so we come down to Rangoon with the sun shining on the golden Pagoda.

The scent of the wood-fires reaches us through the ventilation of the ship, and the flames compete with the roof of the Pagoda for the attention of the afternoon sun.

The Captain comes and tells me that the Rangoon aerodrome is a perfect beast, and, as he goes back to the cockpit to make his landing, I look down and cordially agree with him. It is a nasty, small, knobby, little aerodrome. But we circle and circle round it, sinking all the time, until the critical moment when the Captain drops the ship to the ground within a few yards of the edge, and brings it to rest, as usual, immediately in front of the restaurant.

I will add a line to this before I go to bed. In the meantime I want to stroll round Rangoon.

.　　.　　.　　.　　.　　.　　.

Later. In Rangoon

I took a stroll round Rangoon and tumbled head first into one of the loveliest sights that have ever come my way. It was a very hot evening, and I was drifting very, very slowly along the broad streets, and round a corner I came upon a tree that was almost unbelievable. It was about the size of an ordinary English chestnut, but instead of the heavy green leaves of the chestnut, there was nothing visible except a thick mass of red flowers. Imagine a chestnut all red flowers and no leaves, and you get the sort of idea. And the red was like no other red. It had a sort of yellowish, golden, orange lightness about it, so that it wasn't crimson or scarlet or vermilion or Velazquez. It was a golden red, and that's the nearest I can get to describing it.

I turned another corner and there was a whole street with these trees on each side, leaning over so that you were in the nave of a Gothic cathedral which some fantastic bishop had painted with this mysterious colour.

Did you ever go through Aix-en-Provence when you were whizzing down to the Riviera in the monstrous motor-cars of your still more monstrous friends? If you did, you will remember perhaps — though I think it unlikely — the Cours Mirabeau, the great street which runs, with its overhanging plane-trees, from the statue of Roi René at one end to the Casino at the other. Imagine that in golden red, and you will get some faint idea of what Rangoon can be like. I discovered afterwards that the tree is called the gulmohur.

There are many other colours in Rangoon — the yellow Indian laburnum and its relation, the pink cassia; the amherstia; the gamboge robes of the rascally-looking priests; the magenta dresses of the women; and the English annuals in the gardens of the residential quarter, simple, homely, little flowers like petunias and snapdragons and stocks and daisies. But none of the colours can remotely compare with the gulmohur. Even the gold Pagoda seemed dull in comparison, and the bougainvillea was almost subfusc. I shall always think kindly of Rangoon, although it is very hot, because it first introduced me to that mass of flame. R.

19th April, 1939
Above the Burmese Mountains

I am in a hurry now. Always in long-distance journeys I start slowly and hurry madly towards the end. I suppose there are people who start anything — a job of work or a travel — with a great rush and slacken off and can't finish. I am the other way round. When I see the South Sea Islands within reach, I must gather up my skirts and race towards them.

And this suits my crew very well. India, which they call British India, is just a bore to them. What they are longing to see is the Dutch East Indies, which they call India.

Incidentally, it's a trick which vaguely I resent. — I am no great Imperialist, and I have never put great store upon the far-flung outposts and the dinner-jacket, and the lesser breeds without the law. But vaguely I resent the suggestion that India is not India, but a group of Malayan Islands. However, I say nothing about it to the Steward, for fear that he would give me the history of Van Tromp.

It takes two and a half days to go by sea from Rangoon to Bangkok, and you can't go by train at all. But we are hopping over the mountains, and in three hours we are coming down for breakfast beside the golden towers and the palm woods and the little twinkling canals of Siam.

The whole countryside is marked out with little sunlit ponds, as if a Chinaman had got smallpox. Siam seems to be a country of rivers with forests on each side of them. There are hundreds of little boats moored against the banks, and warships are lying off Bangkok.

I would like to hire a launch and explore those little streams which run past the temples and under the shade of the palms. But I haven't time. The coral lagoons are calling. So a quick breakfast and up again over the rice-fields to the Gulf of Siam, and across the Gulf and across the Malay Peninsula, and over interminable forests, presumably full of white elephants, towards Penang.

The forests are criss-crossed endlessly with inland waterways, but I can't tell from here whether they are rivers or arms of the sea, and off the coast are hundreds of little islands, and everywhere trees. The sea is dead flat and green. Everything is green here. It seems a thousand years since I was over the

Aegean, where everything was blue. The water below is clotted up with green seaweed.

Now we've crossed the Peninsula and we're dropping into Penang. All I know about it is that I used to have some stamps of Penang many years ago. I will write you something about it tomorrow, because I am going to spend the night there in order to avoid the danger of meeting military friends of yours in Singapore.

Later

Penang is a dream of a place. It looks nothing from the airport, but the town and the country round are both enchanting. I wish I could stay here longer. There are remnants of old colonial buildings, solid, rather dilapidated, cream-coloured, with white arches all round the first-floor balconies and gaily painted woodwork, blues and pinks and greens, and everywhere there are flowering trees. In the hotel courtyard there is frangipanni and laburnum, and on the lawn on the edge of the Sound there are enormous tamarisk trees, and the gulmohur is just coming into flower. Little dusky men run up and down the streets pulling painted and patterned rickshaws, without a sound from their bare feet on the hot stones.

This really is a place that seems to have been left behind by the march of progress. Everything is old and rather stately in a queer sort of way. Fort Cornwallis must date from the early nineteenth century, and the guns and mortars along the front of the hotel must have been out of action for nearly a hundred years.

Penang is an island, and I am sitting in an easy-chair on the lawn looking across to the lowwooded coast-line of Malaya and the mountains beyond. At the entrance to the Sound there must be islands, but all you can see from here is the tree-tops sticking out into the sky. Fishing-boats are coming in from the day's work with dark triangular sails, and rowing-boats with six or eight oars come pushing past, while the birds in the tamarisk trees sing little tunes. They don't whistle like ordinary birds, but they distinctly have their tunes.

Later again

After dinner, I went out into the streets and saw hundreds of jolly little brown babies playing in the dust, or curled up sound asleep, or being washed by their mothers on the ground-floor verandahs. Sometimes there was a sudden whiff of incense, and once I tracked down a burst of cheerful music in the hopes of finding some native musicians, only to discover an American gramophone at the end. There are palm trees all over the place, and some of them have red clusters of dates.

I like this place so much that I am going to wait another half-day and take a swing round the island. There are some cheerful Dutchmen in this hotel, and I have just been told that some Scottish planters are coming down from the estates to have their weekly party tomorrow. It may be interesting to meet them and hear something about local conditions.

Telegram from Penang, handed in at 11.30 A.M. the Following Day

The planters came down last night stop Am not feeling well stop Am staying here another day stop Will write to-morrow stop Collect on delivery stop

21st April, 1939
Penang

Those scoundrelly planters came down all right. There was no mistake about that. I never met such a crowd of rascals in my life. I was in their society from lunch-time until some unspecified and unremembered hour this morning, and I can't honestly say that I learnt anything about local conditions. Lunch lasted from half-past twelve until six o'clock in the evening, and then one of them decided that he must go to his tailor's, and that I must accompany him.

We went to his tailor's, and he behaved not exactly in the way that I behave in Savile Row. He sat down beside the counter, summoned the Penang citizen who owned the shop, and announced firmly that he would not discuss business until the tailor had produced a bottle of whisky, a syphon and two glasses.

The tailor produced them, and at a quarter to seven the planter began to talk business. This consisted of insulting the tailor, calling him a cheat, a purveyor of bad cloth, a rotten cutter and, in general, a total loss. By this time every assistant in the shop was standing round screaming with laughter, while we drank whisky and the volume of insults went on. Then suddenly the planter ordered two dozen pairs of shorts and a dozen pairs of white linen trousers, and we left the shop on the best of terms with everyone.

After that he took me to a Chinese dinner where he insulted the restaurant proprietor in such surprising language that we were given the best of everything and were waited on by the proprietor in person. And after that we went on to an enormous night-club.

Here again my Scottish friend seemed to be completely at home. He walked up to the best table on the edge of the dance-floor and sat down. A waiter hurried up and told us that the table was engaged. The planter beckoned to a Chinese girl who was sitting just in front of us. She gave one look at the waiter and said one short sentence which sounded like a cowboy cracking a whip, and the waiter disappeared perspiring.

I asked David — for let us call him David — what had happened and who the girl was, and he explained that she was the top taxi-dancer of Penang. I pointed out that that wasn't much of an explanation, because I had no idea what a taxi-dancer was. He laboriously added to, his explanation that if you wanted to dance you bought a book of coupons, and selected any one of the Chinese girls that you liked the look of, and danced with her and gave her a coupon at the end. So if you danced eight or ten dances with the same girl, the taxi-meter ticked up and you settled at the end with a tip and a packet of coupons.

"This girl," he went on, "is the most famous of them all. She is a personal friend of mine," he wound up, and I am glad to say that he had the grace to blush a little, and that is saying quite a lot of a Scottish planter in Penang.

And about midnight I found myself dancing with the number one taxi-girl. She was very small and very slim, and her dancing was like an autumn leaf fluttering in the wind. My recollection is that you were a very fair dancer in your day, but no European girl could possibly compare with this little Chink. She was exquisite.

Towards the end of the evening David became lachrymose and implored me not to let him go home with the taxi-girl. I pledged him my word that I would do what I could, and at three o'clock in the morning I took him out of the night-club, and got into a cab with him, and drove home to my hotel. But the last thing I saw as I went in, was the flying figure of David racing across the street and jumping into a rickshaw.

I am told that he appeared at lunch today, and was asked what he had done with me last night, and that he replied that he had never even heard of me.

I recovered gradually, after a very bad start, by driving round the island in the fresh air. The bad start was due to a certain — how shall I describe it? — lack of worldliness on the part of a charming Dutch lady who had offered to show me round. I told her rather diffidently that I had been spending the night with these scoundrels, but she obviously didn't grasp the implications, and took me first to see a celebrated temple.

Well, perhaps the temple is celebrated, but it would have done me a lot of good if it hadn't been that its fame rests on the particular thing that it does rest on. The place was full of snakes, lying on the floor, sitting on chairs, coiled round candles, and popping out from behind pictures. I signed the pledge mentally for the hundredth time, and crept gibbering out into the sunshine. At the door a very, very old man said that if I gave him fifty cents he would pray for me, so I gave him a dollar.

But after that things improved. The island is a beautiful place with rubber-plantations and jungly roads and palm trees near the sea, and sudden splashes of colour where a Malay or a Tamil or a Kling trims the edges of the road in a pale-blue skirt or with a scarlet hood over his head. The hibiscus grows wild, and the scents of the jungle mix with the smell of salt fish as a bus loaded with baskets goes down to the market.

After I made my tour, I went to the Botanical Gardens and saw the flowering shrubs — bougainvillea, purple and pink and orange so that they looked like azalea, and the jacaranda which is just like wisteria, and the splendid African tulip-tree, and best of all a variety of cotton-tree which is like the gulmohur only that its flowers are not red but a dark lemon colour. It also flowers without leaves and is quite superb.

And finally I went up the funicular railway to the top of the hill and looked down on the view of the Strait. I have never been — thank God — to Sydney or to Rio de Janiero, so I don't know what their views look like, but I do know that Penang, seen from the terrace of the Residency, beats the Golden Gate of San Francisco, and the Firth of Forth seen from George Street in Edinburgh, and the Bay of Naples, and even the Gulf of Corinth. It's the most beautiful view I have ever seen.

We sat on the balcony of the Residency and drank beer and looked across a hedge of dark blue convolvulus, which is called Morning Glory, and across flower-beds of dahlias and chrysanthemums and orchids growing in the open, and the flower of the passion-fruit, down to this stupendous sight of the Strait of Penang and the shore of Malaya beyond. R.

You are very, very far away.

22nd April, 1939
In the Air Again

And now I am on my last lap of Flight. Sometime today I will reach Java, and I will say goodbye to my Captain and my crew, and I will send my aeroplane back to Holland while I take a ship and disappear for ever.

We flew down the coast of Sumatra, with its endless flat forests and its rivers and its variations of green, past the smoke of oil-refineries and the haunt of elephants and extinct volcanoes on the sky-line. We stopped for a moment at Singapore for petrol, but I didn't leave the aerodrome. There are too many British soldiers and airmen there.

And then from Singapore we started on this last lap, across the shallow seas and the thousand islands. The sea is so shallow that you can see the sand underneath it, like huge jellyfish with ragged edges, the colour of opals. There seems to be no tide, and no surf, and no waves.

And now in the distance I can see Java, and my Dutchmen are getting excited. They are within sight of India. R.

And I am within sight of my coral lagoon.

LETTER XXV

Same Day
Java

This is the most extraordinary place. It is like what every Californian shouts, and what every Californian actually believes, that California is. The trees are greener than anywhere else in the world; the island is the most densely populated for its size of all islands; the crops grow more quickly and more often; the hibiscus is as red as your lips; the folk laugh as easily as they laugh in Montana; there are hedges of vermilion poinsettias; there is running water everywhere; there is the vilest heat in Batavia and the gentlest of cool breezes in Bandoeng, in the hills above; there is rice and tea and coffee and quinine and oil and rubber and tulip-trees and oleander — oh well — I'm not going on about it. The plain fact is that Java has to be seen to be believed.

I was so staggered by it — and so obviously made no secret of the fact that I was staggered — that the Steward was enchanted, and told me a lot about Grotius who seems to have been a Netherlander of some repute in bygone days. The Captain merely purred, and murmured something about Fokker, while Sparks excitedly grabbed his knobs and buttons and sent off a message to his girl in Rotterdam, again at my expense, to the effect that I adored Java and he adored her. I'm right, of course, and he's just a pathetic boob.

But it's a sad business, saying goodbye to these trusty Hollanders. We've only been a few days together — heavens! it is only about a fortnight since I was burning your photographs in my flat in Belgravia and expunging your blue eyes from my heart and my memory for ever — and yet a sort of friendship has grown up between these lads and me which I'll never forget.

I rather think there are two reasons for it — at least, on my side. On theirs, I fancy that they feel well disposed towards me because they think I'm slightly touched in the head. Just as the Red Indians were always civil to loonies instead of scalping them, so these good-humoured Netherlanders smile and pat me on the back as much as to say, "Yes, yes, there's a big boy."

The two reasons why I like them are: (1) They are free and peaceful and sensible and placid (except for Sparks who is madly in love, and the Steward who is a belligerent fighter in the cause of peace), and (2) they are supremely efficient. In the days, far-off days, when I was kneeling at your feet and getting kicked in the mug for my pains, I was, as perhaps you may recall, a sort of artist in a small way. And no one who is an artist even in the most exiguous way can fail to worship efficiency.

There aren't many thrills in life quite so good as watching an expert doing the thing he's expert in — whether it's making a violin, or coming down the Cresta, or going up the Matterhorn.

And these Hollanders are good at the things they're good at — if you follow me. Sparks can tell a volt from an ampere as soon as look at it. The Steward plies a pretty corkscrew; and the Captain, for all his jovial bulk, is the nearest thing to a human butterfly that has alighted on an aerodrome for quite a while.

So I love them, and they tolerate me, and now we must part.

My Charter-Flight is over. I have flown from a Lady.

In a fortnight — what have I seen? The roots of the world. I have seen places where a lot of religions were made — Jerusalem, and Persia, and the neighbourhood of Benares, and Rangoon. I have seen some of history — from Alexandria, which Alexander founded, to the Indus which Alexander reached, and further, and further. I have been to Babylon and beyond. How many miles to Babylon? Four-score and ten. Half an hour for us in our silver dragon. I have dropped down into a civilization here and there. Several towns too, not unimportant in their various ways, have flitted beneath me at two hundred miles an hour. Athens and Naples, and Baghdad and Jericho, and Ajaccio and Marseilles and Singapore and some others.

I have seen a hill or two. The Mountain of the Sainte Victoire, and Vesuvius, Stromboli, Pisgah, Carmel and Hermon, and the high places of Burma and Siam, and the horizon of Sumatra.

But beyond all, surpassing all, I have seen Rivers.

By the Splendour of God, as William the Bastard used to shout, I have seen some Rivers. Listen to the roll of their names, and put a little history beside each one. Thames, I flew down. I crossed the mouths of the Rhine where it's called the Scheldt. The Seine was invisible because of fog, but the tumbling Rhône came out at Avignon. Tiber was a little fellow, but Nile spread out for thousands of acres. The Brook Kedron had no water in it, but it gave a kick to the old heart, and Jordan twisted about among the bones of its ancient lions. Then Euphrates and Tigris, and Indus, and Jumna, and Ganges, and Brahmapootra, and the Irrawaddy, and Bangkok's river whose name I've forgotten, and all the elephant-haunted rivers of Sumatra. What is there left, in all the world, of rivers which I haven't seen in a fortnight?

Let's think. There's the Yang-tse, infested now by yellow Japanese lice. There's the Amazon where you may lose Colonel Fawcett and find Peter Fleming almost simultaneously. The Mississippi, haunt of Edna Ferber, and Mark Twain, and coons, and crooners. The Volga, much used by boatmen and the BBC. And the Vistula. And Abana and Pharphar. And perhaps Belloc's Evenlode. But that's about the lot.

There are a thousand others — Niger, Congo, Colorado. But on how few of their banks has history been linked with the flowing water. Mungo Park was a great man, but his Niger is a dreary trickle when you think of the Cephisus of Athens. And Orinoco is only a resounding name, whereas the Avon is Shakespearean.

I wish I was a poet. Then I could have written something about you which might have done justice to your loveliness, and I could have written something about my Rivers.

But poetry isn't in me, so there is nothing left but to quote a verse or two of a real poet.

Jack Squire, a real poet, the one who wrote about Frasers and Murrays and pig-sticking memoirs, wrote this about rivers:

> And the holy river Ganges,
> His fretted cities veiled in moonlight,
> Arches and buttresses silver-shadowy
>   In the high moon,
> And palms grouped in the moonlight
> And fanes girdled with cypresses,
> Their domes of marble softly shining
> To the high silver moon.
>
> And that aged Brahmapootra
> Who beyond the white Himalayas
> Passes many a lamassery
>   On rocks forlorn and frore,
> A block of gaunt grey stone walls
> With rows of little barred windows,
> Where shrivelled monks in yellow silk
> Are hidden for evermore. . . .

That's the stuff of which immortality is made. And now it is over. My charter-flight in my great Dutch machine is ended. I've escaped — for ever.

I've begun already to negotiate for a small sailing-ship which will take me from Batavia, through the jade, shallow seas, to Sourabaya and thence for home. For that is what I have come to call my lagoon-island — wherever I may find it

— I have come in my mind to call it Home. I wonder if Stevenson had an island in his thoughts when he wrote that piece about the hunter being home from the hill. I shouldn't be surprised.

It will be about three days before my sailing-ship is ready, so I'm going to potter round the island, to fill in time.

Then I'll write to you one last letter, and then goodbye, my pet. And never, never will you hear from me again. R.

My darling crew has left me in tears. We tried to shake hands phlegmatically, but it was no good. The Captain murmured something about a nice trip, and the Steward cursed Torquemada. Sparks tapped out the Morse Code for Love with his fingers on the table. As it was in Dutch, of course, I didn't understand. The Second Pilot gave me a picture-postcard of a Pieter de Hooghe, and the Engineer gave me a spanner, tied with a ribbon of Dutch colours.

24th April, 1939
Batavia

Tomorrow I sail. Everything is ready. I've hired my schooner and my sailors, and I'm off to the islands where Conrad's King Tom Lingard fought for an ideal and was betrayed by Mrs. Travers so that in the end it was once again Belloc's

> A name disherited; a broken sword;
> Wounds unrenowned; battle beneath no Lord;
> Strong blows, but on the void, and toil without reward.

Though in all fairness — my finest quality, perhaps — I must admit that in my calf-like days which came to an end so very recently, I would have done quite a lot for a Mrs. Travers if I'd met her, or anyone like her, in real life.

But she betrayed him none the less and ruined all. And when they met at daybreak upon the sandbank, after the heroes were dead in vain and the trust had been thrown away by a woman, all the words that King Tom could find in his simple heart to conclude the business were, "What has hate or love to do with you and me? Hate. Love. What can touch you? For me you stand above death itself; for I see now that as long as I live you will never die."

The foolish fellow. Or was he?

Anyway, the Shallow Seas are waiting for me and I'll soon put all the Mrs. Travers out of my mind.

When the yacht with the woman on board was sailing back to civilization on the last page of The Rescue, King Tom Lingard was filling the main topsail of his brig and leaning with arms folded and looking down at the evening sea.

His mate, young Carter, comes up to him. "The tide has turned and the night is coming on. Hadn't we better get away from the Shoals, sir?"

"How was the yacht heading when you lost sight of her?" asks King Tom.

"South as near as possible," Carter replies, and then he asks his captain for a course.

And the last words in the book are, "Lingard's lips trembled before he spoke, but his voice was calm. 'Steer north,' he said."

And except that our compass-courses are exactly opposite, our attitude each to our own respective Mrs. Travers is identical.

. . . . . .

During the last three days I've seen lots of things in this emerald isle. I've motored up through dense jungle on each side of the road to the very edge of the crater of a volcano, and looked down at the Malay inspectors creeping about in gas-masks among the sulphur fumes and the sinister, bubbling pools, and the yellow-encrusted lava. Surely this must be a unique trade. These lads test the temperature of the crater every day. If there is a sudden rise, they hop out and warn the locals to beat it.

I've seen woods that are partly blackened by the sulphur and partly festooned with white trumpet-shaped flowers, and a panther dodging across the road to avoid the car, and pools covered with pink water-lilies, and always people and people, everywhere.

I've visited a tea-plantation and driven down the long, grassy alley-ways between the tea shrubs, and a rubber plantation where the only colour to break the everlasting green is the orange bands which have been painted round the good trees so that they won't be cut down when the time for replanting comes along. At the moment there is plenty of colour among the tea because tea needs shade, and the shade is provided just now by a variation of the laburnum, so that the plantations are a cloud of citron flowers. But it won't last, because some busybody scientist has found, or pretends that he's found, that laburnum is bad for tea, so the whole lot are to be uprooted, and some drab tree planted instead.

The manager of the tea estate took me over his factory at breakneck speed, and then we settled down to talk about books. I only had an hour for my visit, but somehow we managed to talk from a quarter of an hour before noon till half an hour after midnight. He was an Irishman, and after we had finished the beer, and then finished the whisky, we came towards evening on an admirable line in brandy-and-soda, while the talk and the laughter thundered and volleyed round the high ceilings of the house.

As we neared the end, a cool wind brought us the mingled scent of sulphur and orange pekoe and the flowers of the woods, and I borrowed a big overcoat from the Irishman for the drive back to Bandoeng. Now that the matter comes into my mind I haven't the faintest idea what happened to that overcoat. I remember distinctly that it kept me very snug in the car, and that I sang a good deal on the way down, in pretty good voice, though I say it as shouldn't. But I never saw it again, and it is at least a thirteen to eight chance that the Irishman never sees it again either.

So back from Bandoeng to Batavia, in an old-fashioned Fokker, noisy, but a nice machine to look out of because it has a top-wing so that you can look straight down. That is the only fault to be found with the Douglas — the low wing is apt to get in the way. When you are longing to get a glimpse of Ctesiphon, it's irritating to find a vast, glistening stretch of metal between you and the Arch.

Two nights in Batavia: on the first, they took me to a very jolly opium den, where fat Chinks showed me how to smoke opium in a tiny cabin plastered with newspaper photographs, a couple of years old, yellow, with a patina of smoke on them, of the Duke and Duchess of Windsor. On that night too they gave me a delicious supper of grilled frogs'-legs, washed down with Dutch beer, and topped up with Kummel, and they took me to a night-club.

But alas! there was no taxi-girl , to compare with the autumn-leaf of Penang who flitted over the dance-floor like a shadow, and who charged a hundred and thirty-five Straits dollars for her favours after the ball was over, and who stroked the inside of your hand with a small alabaster forefinger if she wished to explain that, to people who amused her, favours were free. There was no almond-eyed sylph in Batavia within a thousand miles of Penang's top taxi-girl.

The second evening was memorable, for a Dutchman, formerly a famous cavalry officer who had smashed his leg over a jump, took me to dine at the Harmonie Club.

I wouldn't have thought it possible that any club in the world could have competed with the Byculla. But the Harmonie not merely competes. If it had a compound like the Byculla, it would be well out ahead. For the building is even more beautiful, and the tradition is, I think, even older.

The Harmonie dates from the same sort of period, but its record is longer in continuity. For more than a hundred and twenty-five years its front door has never been closed. For a century and a quarter members have been able to get something to eat and drink at any hour of the day or night.

. . . . . .

Tomorrow I set sail. I shall coast along the north of Java to Sourabaya. There I'll make the final arrangements for stores and so on, and then I'll disappear.

It occurs to me that the voyage to Sourabaya will take about four days, and that I won't have very much to do on board and that, in any case, I owe you a last will and testament.

So maybe you'll hear from me just once more.

R.

Harmonie is the perfect name for a Club in which there are no lady members.

25th April, 1939
Nearing Sourabaya in a Small Sailing-Ship

"Farewell and Adieu to you, fair Spanish Ladies."

This is my last declaration of Faith, my Testament.

I was in love with you from the first moment I saw you — three years ago — until we parted, a fortnight since or thereabouts. There is no secret in that. The world knew it and still thinks that I still am.

But Man has been given one quality, to make up a little for his many disadvantages in a woman-controlled world, which has seldom been given to Woman. He can bring down an iron curtain and black out his past emotions in a moment, if he only is strong enough to make up his mind to do it.

So with me.

The three years no longer mean a thing to me. I have no single tear to shed, no sigh, no regret, no pang at what might have happened if the luck had run the other way, or if the timing had worked out differently, or if you hadn't been you and I hadn't been — I.

It is a clean sheet and a new beginning. The iron curtain is down, and I can look at the three years just as coolly as if they had been lived by someone else.

Were they happy years, I wonder? Or were they miserable? Or were they a bit of both, happiness and misery by turns? It is difficult to say. But one thing is certain. I shall never, never regret them, even though by all worldly standards they have ended in such a resounding tumble of all my pack of hopes and longings.

It isn't ever pleasant to admit that one has concentrated upon a certain object for a thousand days, never slackening the concentration for a single hour of a single one of the days, and that one has failed utterly and completely at the end of it all.

But although it has been such a failure, it was gloriously worth while in a curious sort of way. You may say, "How can it be worth while to throw three grand years of your life into the sea and having at the end to uproot yourself and go to live for ever in outlandish parts? Where is there anything worth while in that?" Reasonable questions — and they'll only get unreasonable answers.

By all the rules, the three years have been thrown into the sea. I admit it. But then I never went by rules. It is only by my own feelings that my own gains and losses can be measured. What is a dead loss to other men mayn't be a dead loss to me. It mayn't even be a loss at all. It's often said, as a sneer, that artists claim a different set of rules and conventions to the ordinary, decent, honest folk, and that they put forward this different set as an excuse for their outrageous actions.

It looks true, but it isn't really true. All they do is to claim the right to judge themselves by themselves.

During the last three years, a hundred charitable souls, thinking only of my welfare, have told me that I was a fool; that grown-up people don't behave like that; that life is too short anyway; that one woman is so like another after you've known her for a year or so that it's absurd to draw fine distinctions between them; that calf-love is one thing that is physiologically explicable, and that senility is another thing that is explicable, but that in between lies the Age of Reason; and so on and so on. One clinching argument which I have listened to courteously a hundred times is that no Frenchman would have behaved as I have behaved. "The French are adult; they understand the world. They know how to live."

All of which, I am sure, is perfectly true by the ordinary set of rules. To me, none of it made sense. I had my own profit and loss account in my mind as they babbled on.

What had it got to do with me if the world thought I was being a child? And why the French? And what is Reason, anyway? There is only one way to judge my three years, and that is by my own thoughts. And no one can do that except myself.

．　．　．　．　．

Of course, a great deal of it was horrible. Obviously it must have been. Being deeply in love with someone who will only see you once a month or so, and then only for an hour or two, is a very poor amusement. And I suppose that is why they all laughed at me. Just a figure of fun. Being deeply in love with someone who goes out day after day with other men because she prefers their company to mine is no joke.

I agree with all that. I'm in an experienced position to agree with all that. I know all about it. But there was more in it.

You never asked me to fall in love with you. Never for one moment did you owe me anything. I am not one of those fools who think that worship puts the Goddess under an obligation. She is there to be worshipped. That is her *métier*.

If, as well, she is gracious and gentle and understanding, so much the more divine. But no one can demand it of her. And if she isn't, it just can't be helped.

I was in love with you. You weren't in love with me.

That is the beginning and end of the story.

And I never had the faintest claim on you. So why should I whine and bay the moon? But I never did. You must grant me that. Besides, there is the other side of the account, which the clowns and wiseacres and men and women of the world, as they are called, could never understand.

The artist must live at the highest pressure always. He must always be ecstatic or suicidal, and the only certain way to be both is to be passionately in love with a woman. The moment he touches the Middle Way, he is lost for ever.

Because, if he is an artist, he cannot be kept away from his work, and he knows — for he knows pretty nearly everything — that his work depends on white-heat flames. White-heat may be high temperature, or it may be ice-cold temperature; scientists say that if a thing is cold enough it can burn just as painfully as boiling-point. And I know that they are right. The only real disaster is 98.4 Fahrenheit, which is normal. There is nothing painful there. It is the temperature at which Brussels Sprouts live. And normality is death to the artist.

But white-heat flames are the essence of the thing, and only a woman can kindle them in the artist.

So it all comes down to the old story.

The artist lives a lonely, miserable life at the best of times. His trade is difficult; he only wants to do the best, and he never reaches the best; he is solitary; he is impatient and bad-tempered, and full of sadness; and he is madly gay to escape from the shadows.

But — and it is a supreme But — he is endowed by God with the one gift which saves all. He knows the secret of the World as human beings have to live it. He knows that there is no life, no happiness, no misery, nor ecstasy, nor suicide, nor great work, nor exquisite beauty, without women.

To him there is nothing so beautiful in God's creation as a woman. Nor is there anything beautiful in God's creation, a moon or a bank of night-scented flowers or an opal or a mist on willow-hung pools, which is not more beautiful if a woman is standing beside him when he looks at it. Women are the Light of the World to poor, small, ignorant men.

But, those of us poor, small, ignorant ones who have managed to understand that essential truth, are not so far beneath the stars after all. We know how humble we are in the darkness, but we also know where the starlight comes from and how clear and golden the starlight is. So we are not entirely lost. There is always Venus in our sky.

Of all men the artist pays to women the deepest tribute, and of all men he asks for the least in return. No. More. He doesn't ask anything. Not even the simplest of all rewards — a kind word, or a small smile, or a kiss of a white hand. He gets his own reward, sometimes in a painful way — admitted — in a horrible way sometimes — admitted — in knowing with complete and utter certainty that he loves her more, far, infinitely far, more than any other man in the world loves her.

It is a reward — though no one else but an artist will understand it. Of course, the artist is a man as well, and so it can be rather hellish, to think of those other swine whose love is so trivial and who get so much for it.

But that feeling never lasts for long. If it did, one would sink straight down to the level of the swine. And if one did, why pretend to artist's rank? The two things don't go together.

No, no, no, the reward, and the real hell, are in my own heart. That is what I started out to say in this last confession of Faith. No one can. tell me what I've suffered in these three years. But then no one can tell me how I've been exalted. I alone know both, and I've measured them both by my own rules and not by anyone else's.

So this is the final verdict. The hell was hell, long, protracted hell, but the heaven, fleeting moments though it was, far outbalanced it. I was in love with the loveliest thing that ever was seen. I was in love with a swift, darting mind. I was in love with a sweetly gay smile, with dark blue eyes, with the palest and slenderest of all fingers, with wit and beauty and heart.

Is not that something in a man's life? Is not that a thing to thank God for? Are there many men who could say the same?

You will have lovers, hundreds. And not one of them, not one, will feel about you as I do — as I did, I mean.

So let us end. I have made my Flight from you. King Tom Lingard and I are steering away from you. Nothing could have saved me but the Air. Nothing could have torn me out of the old life except the tremendous flying and flying and flying. Two hundred miles an hour has re-born me. Two hundred miles an hour have taken me from the crazy life of adoration and misery, and now I am to be a Brussels Sprout on the edge of a slow Pacific sea.

European no more. Artist no more. Lover no more. Neither ecstasy nor suicide play any part now. I have had my day and caught a glimpse of Paradise, and echoed the old tinker of Pimlico, and dreamt of the Walsingham ballad;

But Love is a durable fire,
In the mind ever burning:

Never sick, never dead, never cold,
From itself never turning.

All, all is finished.

You were the most beautiful. You were the most exquisite. You were the
loveliest. You were Ambassadorial Beauty, Beauty Personate, the giver of
Halcyon Days to undeserving men, and to me.

Amen. Adieu and farewell to you. R.

ἀληθεύων ἐν ἀγάπη speaking the truth in love. Do you hear?

Cable from Sourabaya. Same Afternoon. Monday 3 P.M.

Just got your cable stop KLM 'plane leaves this afternoon stop Meet me Savoy
Grill Saturday night eleven-thirty stop Queen of the World I love you. R.